MW01624854

GUARDING SUZIE (SPECIAL FORCES: OPERATION ALPHA)

Guardian Seals: Book 4

NICOLE FLOCKTON

Dear Readers,

Welcome to the Special Forces: Operation Alpha Fan-Fiction world!

If you are new to this amazing world, in a nutshell the author wrote a story using one or more of my characters in it. Sometimes that character has a major role in the story, and other times they are only mentioned briefly. This is perfectly legal and allowable because they are going through Aces Press to publish the story.

This book is entirely the work of the author who wrote it. While I might have assisted with brainstorming and other ideas about which of my characters to use, I didn't have any part in the process or writing or editing the story.

I'm proud and excited that so many authors loved my characters enough that they wanted to write them into their own story. Thank you for supporting them, and me!

READ ON!

Xoxo

Susan Stoker

Suzie Jay, you're on your way and thanks for letting me use your name!

CHAPTER ONE

A red-hot, searing pain pierced Ryan 'Joker' Smith's leg.

"Fuck." His left leg buckled beneath him. Before he could face plant into the mud an arm banded around his waist and pulled him upright.

"I got you, man. Can you walk?" yelled Greg 'Cowboy' Robertson, both of them ducking as another round of shots were fired in their direction.

Ryan gripped his left thigh. "Yeah." Even if he couldn't there was no way he'd let his teammate know.

Cowboy nodded. "We'll get to cover and then we can check out your injury."

Gritting his teeth Ryan shifted most of his weight to his right leg and, with Cowboy's help, they made their way to a grove of trees.

"Sit-rep." Robot's voice came over the coms.

"Joker's hit," Cowboy responded to their leader.

"We're heading to the trees ten clicks west from our last check in. Will give update when we can.'

"Roger, that.'

A few seconds later they were covered by trees and Ryan collapsed on the ground. "Shit, this burns like a fucker."

Cowboy slapped his pack down on the ground next to him and pulled out his first aid kit. "This is gonna burn even more."

Ryan knew what exactly was going to happen next. "Tell me something I don't already know. Where are the other guys?"

"Who the fuck knows. Now get ready."

Cowboy ripped the QuikClot pack and poured the contents over his bullet wound. Ryan bit back a groan at the sting of the powder. He breathed through it, when what he really wanted to do was curse up a blue streak. He knew the QuikClot was only a temporary measure, but it would be enough to get him through until they were able to get safely out of the hellhole they were in.

He closed his eyes and rested his back against the tree trunk, waiting until the burn died down to a more manageable pain level.

"You okay?"

He grunted in response to Cowboy's question. He knew the bullet hadn't gone through. It was still lodged in his thigh which meant he had surgery in his future. Thinking about surgery reminded him of the night he'd spent with the hot nurse he'd met when the team had taken his teammate, Italy's, woman, Erin, to hospital after her kidnapping. Behind his closed eyes, a vision slammed his brain, the hot nurse, her hair spread across the pillow, her mouth open groaning out her release, as they climaxed together.

It had been one night three months ago. They'd agreed on the one night. No numbers had been exchanged, but sometimes he thought about her. More than he'd thought about any of his other hook-ups. Ryan refused to acknowledge that he hadn't even thought about sleeping with another woman since that night.

"I don't think it hit any major arteries," Cowboy said as he pressed his fingers around the wound, interrupting Ryan's stroll through his bedroom memories with arrows of pain. "But, I reckon you'll be headed for surgery."

He trusted Cowboy's diagnosis. He was the guy on the team with the medical training. Plus, it confirmed his own thought.

"I guess so. Where are the others?" The second he finished speaking, rustling sounded nearby. It wasn't the sound of an animal. He may be injured but there was no way he was going to let himself or Cowboy be sitting ducks for the insurgents their special ops team was still in the middle of battling. Ryan raised his rifle ready to shoot the motherfuckers.

"It's us," A voice hissed in his earpiece. A moment later, Carlos 'Italy' Porcelli's face broke through the trees. "You okay, Joker?"

"Fucking peachy. What's happening?"

While they'd been sitting treating his injury, the

unmistakable popping of rapid gunfire had all but disappeared.

"Insurgents are dead, and we've got the hostage. Red and T-Rex are dealing with her." Robot answered as he squatted down beside him. He stretched out his hand and Ryan spied two white pills.

No fucking way was he taking pain pills. "I'm good."

"Take them. We've got transport out arriving in five minutes. Once we get airborne I don't wanna hear your whiny ass complaining?" Robot thrust his hand under Ryan's nose.

Fighting with his team lead wasn't a good idea. Not in the middle of a mission. Without a word, he snatched the pills and dry swallowed them. Once he had, Robot and Carlos framed him and in tandem hauled him up. Ryan slung his arms around them, hating that he had to rely on his teammates to get out to their pick-up point.

He may not be one of the new guys on the team, but he still felt the need to prove himself as an integral part of the team. A shrink would probably say it was a left over hang up from being bullied in high school. He would say it was all part of being a SEAL. But getting shot hadn't been part of his plan.

Cowboy had their back as they threaded their way through the thick mass of trees and foliage to the designated pick up area. The *thwump thwump thwump* of a black hawk helicopter grew louder, and they broke into the clearing as the bird hovered above them.

The pills started kicking in, dulling the pain and his senses at the same time. He glanced to the right and saw a woman dressed in clothes that had seen better days. Her top was ripped and covered in mud. The pants she wore also bore numerous tears. He clenched his fists, hoping she hadn't been sexually assaulted while she'd been in captivity.

T-Rex hauled her close to him as the ladder was dropped from the 'copter. One by one the team climbed up. Italy went to grab Ryan's pack, but he shook the other man off.

"I've got this," he ground out. No matter how much pain the next twenty seconds were going be, he had no plans to show any weakness in front of the guys.

Ryan gripped the rope and heaved his leg up onto the first rung. Pain ripped down from his injury to his ankle, but he pushed it away. Putting one foot after the other he made his way up until the opening yawned before him.

A pair of hands hoisted him up into the machine. He limped over to a seat, sweat pouring down his face as he willed himself not to pass out or throw up, or both, in front of those already seated.

"What happened?" A rough voice next to him asked.

Ryan lifted his eyelids and looked to the left where a man with a wicked scar on his face sat. "Gunshot to the left thigh."

The other man looked at his leg and nodded. "QuikClot appears to be doing its job."

"Yeah." The last thing he wanted was to make polite conversation with a guy he didn't know.

"Truck's the name."

Ryan sighed, okay, the guy wanted to chat. "Joker."

The helicopter dipped forward once everyone was onboard, and Ryan looked around to find other unfamiliar guys seated in the small area. Like the guys on his team, their faces were smeared with black paint. Unlike his team, who were dressed in camos, these men were dressed in head-to-toe black. Their demeanor indicated they weren't another SEAL team. They were more than likely an elite forces squad, and he knew better than to ask who they were and what they'd been doing.

Another look around showed him there didn't appear to be another hostage on board, so they may have been in the same location on a recon mission or had completed their task and were on their way back to a base so they could head home.

He shifted and winced at the pain. It was going to be a long ride home.

Seventy-two hours later, Ryan was lying in a hospital bed in Virginia waiting for a doctor to clear him so he could go home. The whole helicopter ride and subsequent surgery had all passed in a blur.

The door opened, and he hoped like hell it was the doc with release papers in his hand. Instead a tall, willowy nurse walked in. His eyes were half open, feigning sleep. She looked vaguely familiar. There was something about the tilt of her head that teased a memory in his mind. His body stirred to life as she got a little closer. The scrubs did nothing to hide the generous swell of her cleavage, nor the curve of her ass.

Great, just what he needed, a woody when he was dressed in a stupid hospital gown that exposed half his ass and was thinner than a tissue. A fresh rose scent assailed his senses, blanking out the antiseptic smell of the hospital.

The hidden memory roared to life. He recognized the scent. He'd inhaled it deeply when he'd trailed kisses along a silky-smooth shoulder. When he'd caressed the most perfect breasts he'd ever seen. When he'd had the best orgasm of his life.

"Roses," he muttered.

"Oh, you're awake. How are you feeling?"

There was nothing in her voice indicating she recognized him. He ran the hand not attached to an IV over his face and connected with the bristles covering his chin and cheeks. The time they'd been together he'd been clean shaven. Maybe that's why she didn't recognize him. Or he'd totally mistaken his nurse as the same one he'd hooked up with. "Ready to get out of here."

"We'll have to see what the doctor has to say about that." Her cool fingers closed over his wrist and fired darts of pleasure through his body. His dick hardened even further, and he shifted so his erection wasn't obvious beneath the blankets.

This nurse had to be the same one he'd spent the night with. His body had responded the same way the night they'd had dinner. "It's Suzie, isn't it?"

The pressure from her fingers against his wrist tightened for a fraction of second before going back to their previous tension. "Is what Suzie?"

"Your name. You're Suzie Waterson."

Her fingers released his arm and she made some notes on the clipboard in her hand. "If this is a pickup line, it's not very original, Einstein. I'm wearing a name tag."

"The name's Joker, not Einstein."

The clipboard she held clattered to the ground. Yep, she remembered him.

Suzie squatted down and used the few seconds it took to pick it up to gather her thoughts. Her heart-rate tripled its normal rhythm. This couldn't be happening. Not now. The last person she expected to see was the man she'd had a one-night stand with three months ago lying in a hospital bed.

The man who was the father of the baby she carried.

A man she never thought she'd see again. Although she'd known, at some point, she'd have to try and locate him to let him know he was a father. She figured it would be a few years down the track.

"Are you okay down there? Do I need to find a doctor for you, Roses?"

Roses. What the heck did he mean by that.

Breathing deeply, she gripped the board tightly against her chest and stood up, a smile pasted on her face. "My name is Suzie, not Roses and it's been a little while since I've seen you—" She glanced down at the chart for his name. No way was she going to call him Joker, even though that was the name she'd called out numerous times the night they spent together. "—Ryan. I would ask what you're doing here, but it's pretty obvious."

A gunshot wound to the thigh. He had been extremely lucky the bullet hadn't nicked the femoral artery.

"Roses, because that's the scent you wore the night we were together and you're it now. How have you been?" he asked. His voice as smooth as ice cream sliding down her throat.

Her face flushed at why he was calling her *Roses*, and she couldn't stop the bubble of desire forming in her blood.

It had always been that way, since the first time she met him when he'd come in with a couple of women who'd been kidnapped. Working at a hospital in Virginia she was used to seeing military personnel coming and going. But the second Ryan and his team had walked in all the nurses had swooned a little. Even with her vow to stay clear of men who gave off alpha vibes, she'd been drawn to him. The corny jokes he'd told as he flirted with her had her laughing and before she'd known it she'd agreed to have dinner with him. At the time she'd had no idea which branch of the military he'd belonged to. He'd told her he was a SEAL over dinner and the cloak of danger that surrounded him made sense. He'd also explained he was called Joker because of his joke telling skill. She kind of figured that out herself as she didn't think anyone would name their kid *Joker*.

"I've been good. Busy. You know how it is. You get up, go to work, go home, go to sleep. Rinse and repeat." Oh God, could she stop babbling? She never babbled. Seeing Ryan again had thrown her for a loop. There was a reason she hated rollercoasters, all those unexpected loops where your stomach falls into your throat and you think it's never going to return to its proper position.

Clearing her throat Suzie concentrated on checking the rest of Ryan's vitals and getting out of there as quickly as she could. "Well, everything looks good," she said as she made a final notation on his chart. "I'll check to see what's holding up Dr. Morton. I'll see you around, Ryan."

Suzie escaped quickly from the room and rested her back against the wall beside his closed door, her heart racing so fast she'd be beeping all over the place if she was attached to a heart monitor.

She couldn't regret falling into bed with Ryan. No matter how many times since she'd told herself it was a mistake. He'd treated her like a princess and, after her ex-husband who'd dominated her in every aspect of her life, including the bedroom, she'd fallen under

Ryan's spell, but they'd agreed on one night only. Now the consequences of that night grew in her belly. Fate had literally thrown Ryan at her mercy. All she had to do was tell a man she'd known for less than twenty-four hours that he was going to be a father.

Didn't that just take the cake?

Suzie lifted her hand and paused. The second she knocked on the eight foot slab of wood she was setting herself on a path of no return. She'd argued with herself so often over the last couple days. Did she tell him? Didn't she tell him? What if he didn't believe her? What if he threw her out on the street? At the end of it all her decision had been—she couldn't keep it from him.

It didn't matter that she'd planned to travel this new path fate had set her on by herself. After tonight she could still be traveling it alone or she could have someone walking alongside of her. The only way she'd ever know is by telling him.

She ignored the shiver of this-is-a-bad-idea rattling through her. Deep inside she knew it was the right thing to do, the only thing. If the hospital found out she'd written down a patient's address, she'd be out of a job.

God knows, she needed her job now.

It had been two days since Ryan had gotten released from the hospital. Two days to build up the courage to break the news to him. How the hell was he going to react? They'd been careful. He'd suited up and she figured she was in the safe zone of her cycle. Guess that tiny print on the condom box was correct when it stated it wasn't one hundred percent foolproof, and she hadn't been in her safe zone after all.

Closing her eyes, she rapped her knuckles on the door. The complex Ryan lived in wasn't fancy. From the outside it appeared serviceable. The exact type of place a bachelor would live in.

Seconds passed and she couldn't hear any noticeable sound to indicate Ryan was home. She should probably go. It was a bad idea in the first place. She'd already decided to go it alone with the pregnancy. She needed to keep it that way. Besides, Ryan was a SEAL his job was dangerous, proof of that was his stay in hospital with a bullet wound. For her sake, and sanity, it would be best if she turned tail and walked away.

Once again, fate had a different idea and the door opened as she was about to walk away.

"Roses? Is that you?"

Any greeting lodged in her mouth at the sight of a bare-chested Ryan standing in the doorway. Well, standing was not quite what he was doing, leaning would be a more accurate description. Sweat beaded across his brow and tension etched the fine lines bracketing his mouth.

Her nursing training kicked in. "You're in pain. You should be resting not standing in the doorway." Not waiting to be asked in, she stepped over the threshold and hooked an arm around his waist.

Heat rocketed through her and she was transported back to the moment when Ryan entered her body for the first time. The connection between them had been instant and simmered until it burst to life in bed.

Now is not the time to be remembering your one night stand. You're here to tell him about the consequences of that night. Not play nursemaid which may or may not include another visit to his bed.

Great now a voice inside of her was playing angel and devil.

"What are you doing?" Ryan asked.

"Helping you so you can lie down. You were shot, and you shouldn't be standing up. You could be doing damage to your wound."

"Wouldn't helping me lie down mean we should be moving, not standing in the doorway with your hand running up and down my back?"

Suzie immediately stopped the unconscious movement of her hand. "Right, let's go," she said, using her *don't mess with me* nurse voice.

"Uh huh."

Together they shuffled down the short hallway and into the room Ryan indicated. He collapsed gratefully onto the couch. Suzie squatted down beside him and grabbed his wrist, her fingers finding his pulse.

"I'm fine. You don't need to make a fuss."

She held up her hand to silence him and concentrated on the *thump thump thump* of his heartbeat. It was a little faster than a normal, but understandable considering the exertion of answering the door and getting back to the couch.

Releasing his wrist, she placed her hand against his forehead to see if there was any indication of a fever. Infection from his wound could still occur. What she wanted to do was check his injury. Make sure the dressing was still in place.

Ryan had left the hospital before he should've. Typical male. They hated to look weak, and being a Navy SEAL he was even less likely to follow doctors instructions and rest. They were known for their *I'm okay, it's just a scratch* attitude. He'd been very lucky, but he wouldn't see it that way. In all likelihood, he would believe he'd let his team down by getting injured. She'd seen more than her fair share of wounded soldiers at the hospital. Each one would rather bleed out than let their team down.

She'd heard the gossip about a team of Deltas who'd saved the life of a man not on their team. How one of the Delta's had clamped his fingers around a vein in the injured man's arm so he wouldn't bleed out.

Every day she heard miracle stories and she couldn't be prouder working in the West Military hospital in Virginia.

Of course, that also meant she put up with a lot of testosterone and alpha males. After being married to a domineering man who made every decision for her, her friends had thought her mad to take a job in such a place. The difference between her ex and the soldiers she tended, they had an undeniable honor her ex-husband had seriously lacked.

The last thing she needed to be doing was thinking about her former marriage while the father of her child lay half naked on a couch in front of her.

Suzie looked up and found Ryan studying her intently.

"Why are you here, Suzie?" he winced as he attempted to sit up a little straighter.

What was the bet he'd not taken any painkillers since he returned home? She'd make a quick buck if there was such a bet. "When was the last time you took some pain meds? And you should still be in the hospital not at home."

"The meds made me nauseous and I don't need them. Pain is manageable. Hospitals suck."

She mentally rolled her eyes, unsurprised at his comment. "Right. Sure, it's manageable. That's why you were sweating and looked like you were about to pass out when you answered the door. And hospitals don't suck. They help you when you're injured. Which you are?"

"Whatever." He dismissed her with a wave of his hand.

She should walk out and leave him to wallow in his pain. It's what he deserved with his dismissive attitude. She'd seen the flash of relief in his eyes when he sat down. No matter how obstinate he was being she was going to stay. Maybe now wasn't the time to break the news that he was about to become a father.

Perhaps it would be better if she waited until he was feeling a little better.

Procrastinator. You know you have to tell him.

Oh boy, that voice needed to be slammed down and locked away. Why hadn't it been so vocal when she'd been stuck her marriage? Because she hadn't wanted to listen to the warnings her friends kept giving her. She was *in love* and knew Peter better than her friends did. Thank God, when it all fell apart her friends had not once said *I told you so* to her face. Behind her back when they'd gotten together without her, no doubt they had. But being her friends, they'd propped her up and supported her until she was back on her feet and divorced.

What would've happened if her parents hadn't died when she was eighteen? For so long she'd fumbled through her grief, managing to get her degree in nursing and then falling in love with Peter.

A hand cupped her jaw dragging her back to the present.

"You look so down, Roses. What's wrong?"

She didn't deserve his concern, not when she was about to blow his ordered world apart. She should go. The last thing Ryan wanted, or needed, was a child from a one-night stand. Suzie couldn't do that to him though. It wouldn't be fair, even if it had been her initial plan.

"I'm pregnant."

CHAPTER TWO

Time slowed. He could see Suzie's lips moving, but he wasn't hearing anything. Had he fallen into a trance? The pain radiating from his leg was fucking unbelievable, worse than after getting shot. Ryan hadn't lied when he told her the meds made him feel like he was about spend an inordinate amount of time hunched over the toilet bowl. But puking up his guts seemed a pretty good option now.

"Stop." He held up his hand. "Back up a bit. Did you just say you're pregnant?"

Suzie's face paled and he wondered if he needed to rush her to the bathroom. Not that he'd be able to do that with is leg, but there was no way he'd be able to cope if she'd tossed her cookies on his hardwood floor.

He also had his answer. She hadn't been trying to shock him into agreeing he should've stayed in the hospital longer. "Shit," he slumped against the cushion. "This can't be happening."

"I'm sorry, Ryan. I didn't mean to dump it on you."

"You coulda fucking fooled me." Anger simmered through him, eating away at the shock.

She sat a little straighter next to him as though his anger was hitting her. "I never expected to see you again. I never expected anything to come of our night together. But it did and then you were admitted to the hospital. I thought you should know about it."

"Right. So, if I'm hearing you correctly you had no plans to ever tell me that I was going to be a father." He ran a hand over his head, his hair a little longer than he normally kept it.

"Not quite."

"In other words, no."

She opened her mouth to protest but closed it again, her shoulders slumping.

Bingo.

"How did this happen, Suzie, it's not like we weren't careful?" God, a pain in his head now thumped a dual beat with his wounded leg.

"I'm sorry, Ryan. I don't know what happened. One of those things I guess. We feel into that unlucky percentage where birth control fails for an inexplicable reason."

Not what he wanted to hear, but no truer words had been spoken. "What do you want to do now? I'm guessing, by your visit, that you plan to proceed with the pregnancy."

She reared back as if he'd struck her across the face. Shit, he wasn't suggesting she terminate. That's the last thing he'd ask a woman to do. It was her body and her life that was going through a major upheaval, more than his would.

"Stop whatever it is you're thinking," he interrupted her again. "I wasn't suggesting you should have a termination. I was just … fuck, I don't know what I'm trying to say here. I can't think straight. Between the pain in my leg, my head and your news I'm pretty sure I stepped into an alternate universe."

"It's a lot to take in. I've at least had a couple months to get over the shock."

He side-eyed her. "Why are you being so reasonable to me right now, when seconds before you were about to rip my head off because of what I said?"

"You're in pain. And shock. I'm not completely heartless." Her hand rested against his forehead again. His eyes drifted shut and the coolness of the touch was blissful against his heated flesh. Exhaustion clawed at him and if any of his teammates saw him like this, they'd either kick him off the team or give him a hard time for letting a bullet wound beat him.

"This is more than just pain, you're dealing with Ryan. I think you're running a fever?"

"It's just hot in here. I need to turn the A/C up." A smile tugged at the corner of his mouth hearing her huff of breath. He didn't need to open his eyes to see the frustration on her face. He didn't think he would be able to anyway, his eyelids seemed to be sewn shut.

"Ryan? Open your eyes?" Hands grabbed him by

the shoulders and jolted him until he forced his eyes open.

"Wha, Isawake." What the heck? The words sound perfect in his mind, but they came out slurred.

"Of course, you're awake. Come on I think you need to go lie down."

He raised his hand to her face, but it fell uselessly down again. "Roses, is that an invite?"

"No. Now come on, up you get."

Ryan attempted to stand, only his legs appeared to be made of rubber and standing was nigh on impossible. He knew this couldn't be good. He'd been able to move and answer the door. Now his body was reacting as it had at the end of BUD/S training, refusing to obey any command to move.

An arm wrapped around his waist and hoisted him up. "Wow, you're strong," he commented.

"I'm a nurse, I've been known to maneuver patients three times my weight. Now where's your room?"

A tiny part of his brain was still coherent, enabling him to take back a bit of his weight, burning pain radiated up and down his leg, more intense than a few minutes ago. He groaned and leaned back on Suzie, who staggered before righting herself. There was a niggling thought floating through his brain, reminding him that he needed to be careful with Suzie. For the life of him he couldn't grasp why it was so important.

Together they stumbled out of his small living room, down the hallway and into the only bedroom the apartment boasted. An instant later he was lying on his bed.

He groaned in relief when the pain subsided in his leg. Hands landed on the button of his jeans. "Baby, all you have to do is ask." He brushed the hands away, popping the button and pulling the zipper down. He was commando so the cool air hit his semi-erect cock. "See all ready."

"Not tonight, Soldier Boy."

"Aww, why not?" There was a tug on his jeans and he lifted his ass to help with the removal of the denim.

"Oh shit."

"Like what you see, huh?" He smiled. Well, he thought he smiled, he had no idea if his body was reacting to the instructions his brain was sending him.

"No, I don't. And stop thinking with your dick."

"Roses, we think with our dicks. It's in our DNA."

"So is stupidity and stubbornness. Your wound is infected. Hell, Ryan, you should've stayed in the hospital."

"Hate hospitals," he grumbled.

"Yeah, again typical male response. Damn, you SEALs are all the same. Never wanting to show any sign of weakness."

"Weakness gets you killed."

"And so will this infection if you don't get it seen to."

His eyes were shut, but his hearing wasn't impaired and the telltale sound of drawers being opened filled the room. Soft cotton landed on his chest as he was about to ask what was going on.

"Put those on. I'm about to call 9-1-1 for an ambulance."

"Don't need no ambulance," he grumbled as he pried his eyelids open to pull on a pair of boxers.

"Don't argue."

Shit, her tone could rival his Commander's *not impressed* voice. Once he had his boxers on he collapsed back on the bed. Lethargy gripped every single muscle in his body. "I think I might sleep."

He succumbed to the blackness.

An annoying *beep beep beep* seeped into Ryan's consciousness. He reached out to slap his hand down his bedside table to eradicate the sound, but connected with fresh air. His mouth was drier than the time he'd been stuck in an Iraqi dessert and they only had two full water canteens left among the team. Rationing water was never fun, but necessary when extraction was still two days away. He shifted but movement in his left leg was restricted due to a heavy bandage.

A hazy recollection of memories presented themselves in his mind. Suzie arriving at his place. Them talking on the couch. Being in his room. Then the bustle of people and him being carted out on a gurney and placed into an ambulance. The agony when the doctor pressed his wound.

He blinked his eyes open. Gazing back down at

him was a row of rectangular ceiling tiles, interspersed with dull fluorescent lights.

Fuck, he was back in the hospital.

"So, sleeping beauty awakens. How are you feeling?"

A familiar face blocked his picturesque view. He'd much rather have woken to that vision instead of a what he had.

He opened his mouth, but nothing came out. With his throat so parched, talking wasn't easy.

"Wait a sec." A low buzz filled the room. The back of his bed began to rise taking him from a reclining position to a semi-upright one. He closed his eyes as a touch of dizziness washed over him.

"Here, take a sip." A plastic straw was placed between his lips and he gulped down the sweet nectar of water.

"That's enough, you don't want to drink too much."

"Are you always this mean, Roses?" he husked out.

"Only with difficult patients," she said with a smile, taking the sting out of her words. "You probably have a few questions."

He sighed. He was back in hospital, and by the feel of the bandage around his leg, it was going to be a while before he was back on active duty. God, he hated showing any type of weakness. "What happened?"

"How much do you remember?" she asked.

"Hey, aren't you supposed to be answering my questions not asking them?"

Suzie rolled her eyes but pulled a chair closer to the bed and sat. He wouldn't have objected to her popping her cute ass on the bed beside him. Then again, it probably wasn't an appropriate action for a nurse to do that with a patient. However, not all patients had seen their nurse naked and knew exactly how to make them cry out in ecstasy. Who knew pale green scrubs could be so sexy?

Beneath the blankets his dick twitched. *Down boy, so not the time.*

"Is your mind back in the gutter, soldier boy?"

He grinned. "You know me so well, Roses."

She chuckled, the sound rolling over him like an ocean wave. "We had one night together. I don't know you that well."

"Well, enough to be pregnant with my baby."

A light pink hue bloomed on her cheeks. "You remembered."

Yeah, he remembered her announcement. His hope that it had been a fever induced memory was squashed in that instant. "How long have I been out?"

"A day and a half."

Not as long as he thought it might have been. Still a day and half where he didn't remember anything wasn't a fun feeling. "I have a vague recollection of you saying my wound was infected. I'm surprised because when I had a shower before you arrived, it was sore but looked fine to me."

"Infections can be insidious, striking when you least expect it. It's probably been festering for a little bit. If you'd been in hospital, we may have detected it earlier and increased your antibiotic dose. You've been taking all your meds haven't you? Well, apart from pain meds, I only had to look at your face when I arrived the other night to see you were in pain."

Shit, do they issue nurses and SEAL Commanders with *don't bother denying anything I can see right through you* looks? Suzie's eyebrows quirked in question and she drummed her fingers on her knee. "Fine. No, pain meds make me nauseous, and I thought the antibiotics were overkill," he admitted.

"Antibiotics were overkill, huh?" She quirked her eyebrow at him. "Still think that now?"

He was choosing to ignore answering the question, particularly when it was obvious how it turned out. He accepted he'd been pigheaded and obtuse about taking antibiotics, but the last thing he was ever going to do was admit that to Suzie. "How long will I be laid up this time."

"Well, if you listen to the doctors and don't discharge yourself before you should be. I imagine you'll be here for a week."

A week? Fuck, I can't be away from the team for that long. No way can they be a man down.

"I see that's causing you some issues," she said before reaching out and laying her hand over his. His flesh warmed beneath hers. What would she do if he turned his hand over and entwined his fingers with hers? Instead he pulled his hand away. A flash of hurt crossed her face and she pushed her chair further back from the bed.

Yep, he was an asshole, but she wouldn't understand. By being laid up for over a week he was letting his team down. His brothers.

"I'll tell the doctor you're awake so he can come and basically tell you what I've told you, but you'll probably take it better from him, because he's a man and not a woman like me."

"What?" The word burst out of him. "That's the last thing I mean. I'm a SEAL. I'm a stubborn asshole. The reason I'm where I am is because I didn't listen to the doctor."

"Whatever, I need to start my shift anyway. I'll see you around, Ryan."

She was out the door before he had a chance to argue further with her. As the door clicked shut, realization struck, they still hadn't talked about her pregnancy. He knew why he was avoiding talking about it —he'd been unconscious for a day and half since she shared her news. What was her reason? Whatever it was, the next time he saw her, he was going to lead off with it.

They were having a child together, and as unplanned as it was, no way was he going to walk away from his responsibility. No matter what Suzie wanted.

CHAPTER THREE

Suzie inserted her key into her lock when the door down the hallway creaked open. Her eyes closed, and she braced for the moment Jeffrey called out to her. Damn her timing, if only she'd got caught at that traffic stop two blocks before her apartment complex. Or she'd left work five minutes earlier, she would've missed him coming out his door. Although, it wouldn't have mattered if any of those scenarios occurred, Jeffrey would exit his apartment the minute she arrived at her door.

At first, she'd thought it was co-incidence. Now it was becoming creepy.

"Suzie, hey, how are you?" he asked as he walked closer to her.

How can he sound so nice and yet creep me out at the same time?

She pasted a smile on her face and faced him. "Hi Jeffrey, I'm good. Glad to be home."

"Tough day at the hospital?"

Dealing with an ornery, stubborn SEAL, not to mention all the other hard-headed military personnel she tended to on a daily basis, yeah it was tough. But she wouldn't change her career for anything. She loved working in the military hospital. The sacrifices the men and women made kept her safe. Except from exasperating neighbors. Maybe if she was rude to Jeffrey instead of nice, he'd leave her alone.

Unfortunately, her mother and grandfather instilled politeness in her, which was why she tolerated bad tempered Navy SEALs and annoying neighbors. "Yeah, it was hard, but I knew that when I chose this occupation." She made a motion to turn the key, hoping he'd take the hint and keep walking to wherever he was headed. "I'll see you around."

She waited half a heartbeat then unlocked the door for real and opened it enough so that she could slip through the door. Once closed, she leaned back against the wood and waited until she heard him retreating from her door.

She tossed her keys into the bowl on the hall stand and walked to the kitchen, exhaustion nipping at her heels. Thank goodness she was getting close to the end of her first trimester and should be getting more energy. It also meant she'd be starting to show soon. Her hand went to her belly and rubbed it.

"Hey, baby, what do you feel like for dinner?" She jumped when her phone rang, then laughed at herself. "Yeah, like the baby is calling you from your belly."

Suzie extracted her phone, frowning when she

didn't recognize the number being displayed. Should she send it to voicemail? No, she didn't get a lot of calls and when she did most were from sales people. But, hey, she had a phone call. "Hello?"

"Suzie? It's Joker –uh—Ryan."

"Oh hey." So the last person she expected to hear from. And how the hell did he get her number?

"I suppose you're wondering why I'm calling and how I got your number?"

Shit, was the guy is a mind reader?

"Yeah the thought crossed my mind."

His chuckle echoed down the line, and her stomach flip-flopped, definitely not the baby doing somersaults, it was way too early for that to occur. "I have a friend who's able to get information."

"Right. And what other information did this *friend* get for you?"

"Only the number, and well, your address."

Creepy much?

"I'm sorry," he spoke softly. "I suppose I should've asked you and not gone behind your back."

How is this any different from you checking his personnel file, grabbing his address and turning up at his house?

She sighed. No way could she make him feel guilty for something she'd done herself. The damn voice in her head wasn't going to let her get away with it either.

"Shut up," she muttered.

"What?"

"No, sorry, I was talking to myself." Mortified she'd spoken her thoughts out loud. She was really losing it tonight. First, thinking Jeffrey was being super stalkerish when he was, in all essence, being a friendly neighbor. And now, talking out loud.

"Talking out loud can get you into trouble sometimes. Anyway, again, I'm sorry that I didn't have the guts to ask you for your number when you were in my room today."

"Honestly, Ryan, it's fine." Suzie couldn't let him continue thinking he was the only who'd used whatever means necessary to get information they wanted. "Did you ever wonder how I turned up at your place, unannounced?"

"You got my address from the hospital."

She shook her head. Of course, he'd work out where she got his address from. The guy was a SEAL, nothing would get past him. "Right. And you didn't have a problem with my invading your privacy. Going against hospital policy?"

A beat of silence passed between them. Suzie would bet half her wage he'd never considered what she'd done as unethical, or against the rules.

"That was a big risk. You could've lost your job if someone found out."

Dread washed over her, he wasn't planning on reporting her, was he? "Yes. Are you planning to snitch on me?"

He laughed again. "No. Your secret is safe with me."

God, she could get used to that sound. Which was absolutely crazy, the guy lived a dangerous life. Hell, he'd got shot and could've died if the bullet's trajectory was three millimeters to the left of where it entered his leg. A sobering thought if there ever was one. The enormity of her decision to keep quiet about the baby weighed down on her like a sack of oranges. She'd known for two months now she was going to be a mom. Her selfishness could've denied her child the chance to know his or her father.

How could she have been so insensitive?

"You could've died," she whispered. "You would've never known that you were going to be a father."

"Aww, hell, Roses, don't say that. It's okay. It's not like we're a couple and this was a planned pregnancy or anything. It's your body and your choice."

"Why are you being so reasonable?"

If she'd kept something this big from her ex, he'd have lectured her for hours about how keeping secrets between husband and wife wasn't the way to a strong marriage. She'd been so stupidly naïve back when they'd gotten married. She'd had stars in her eyes and had watched one too many bridal shows. She'd wanted the dream but instead she'd gotten a nightmare.

"Damn, I wish I could see your face," Ryan said. "This isn't a conversation we should be having on the phone."

On the phone was the best place for this conversation, she wanted to counter back to him. Behind the anonymity of a cell phone she could be brave and say what she wanted. Face to face confrontations were her nemesis. No way could she vocalize what she wanted to say to Ryan's face. After so many years with Peter demeaning her with hidden barbs tied up in ribbons, having serious face to face conversations had her breaking out in hives.

"I suppose we do need to talk," she conceded.

"It's been a crazy couple of days, hasn't it?"

"Crazy couple months more like it."

"You don't know how much I want to hug you and make you feel better, Roses."

Suzie glanced at her watch and saw they'd been chatting for a half hour and she was beginning to feel a little lightheaded. "I need to eat, Ryan. I'll see if I can pop in and check on you tomorrow."

"Okay. I really wanted to check to see that you got home okay."

She rolled her eyes, like he had any need to check up on her. "And yet you never asked me if I was home."

"Huh, I guess I didn't. So are you home or are you out."

She held her phone away from her ear for a few seconds before bringing it back. "Does it sound like I'm out somewhere?"

"Yeah okay, point taken. I'll see you tomorrow then?"

"If I can make it there."

"Sleep well, Roses…and little rose." His voice dropped on those last words.

"Bye," she whispered and disconnected the phone. Tears welled in her eyes. Damn pregnancy hormones.

Yeah blame it on those and not Ryan's sweet farewell to their unborn baby.

The guy was supposed to be a one-off thing, not the beginning of a future. Yet here she was, knocked up and getting all emotional when he said a simple goodbye.

Suzie headed over to the couch and slumped down into the soft cushions. Why was she even letting Ryan get to her? When she'd received the papers confirming her marriage from hell was over, she'd vowed never, ever to let a man control her thoughts and her life. Ryan wasn't doing that by any stretch of the imagination—yet. The guy was a SEAL. There was no way he wasn't going to want to take charge of the situation they now found themselves in. He wasn't the type of guy who would sit back and be happy with someone else calling all the shots when it came to something as important in his life as a child.

What she had to do was make sure she maintained control over her life. It had been a long battle and she'd fought hard and won, and she wasn't going to give it away over an event that ended up with consequences neither one of them ever saw happening.

Suzie shook her head in disbelief at the situation she found herself in. No way could there be a future with Ryan, how many one-night stands turned into forever? They were called that for a reason.

Her head thumped and her stomach churned. She needed food but getting off the couch to cook was the last thing she wanted to do. If she didn't eat, she'd likely spend the rest of the night feeling nauseous.

Dragging herself off the couch she headed for the kitchen, pausing in the hallway when her doorbell rang. Surely it wasn't Jeffrey bugging her again, having to deal with him was the last thing she wanted.

She glanced through the peephole and saw a delivery person holding a white plastic bag. Slipping the lock chain in place, something she should've done the moment she walked through the door, she opened it. "Hi there, I think you have the wrong house. I didn't order any food."

The guy looked at the piece of paper stapled to the back. "Are you Suzie Waterson?"

"Yes."

The guy thrust the bag toward the small gap. "That's the name on the receipt. It's all paid for, tip included."

What the hell? She knew for a fact she hadn't placed an order for any type of food. The aroma wafting from the back had her stomach rumbling in anticipation for whatever was in the sack. "Are you sure?"

He sighed heavily. "Look, lady, this order is for you. I've got other orders to deliver. Give it away if you don't want it. I don't care. My job is to deliver it and I've done that." He placed the bag on the ground and started to walk away before stopping and turning back. He reached into his back pocket and pulled out a folded piece of paper. "Oh, I'm supposed to give this to you."

In a daze, she took the piece of paper from his hand. She popped it in her pocket then closed the door, loosened the chain before re-opening it and picking the bag up.

The paper burned in her pocket as she walked to her compact kitchen, placing the bag on the counter she stared at it for a few seconds. Whatever was in the bag wasn't going to explode, but still she hesitated in reaching in to examine the contents.

Another grumble from her stomach and a wave of nausea washed over her. She needed to eat. Food was sitting in front of her. Food she hadn't had to cook. Food she had no idea where it had come from.

"You are being ridiculous, just open the friggin' note and find out."

Annoyed with the way she was acting, Suzie snatched the note from her pocket and opened it.

Hey Suzie,

I swear I'm not a stalker, but I ordered you dinner. I would've asked you out, but I'm kind of laid up at the moment. I remembered you liked Chinese. I didn't know if any type of food made you feel sick, so I just went with a chicken fried rice and some egg rolls.

Enjoy your meal.

Ryan.

Suzie read the note a couple of times, not quite comprehending that Ryan had done something so thoughtful.

Tears welled up in her eyes and she couldn't stop them from falling. Not once in her marriage had Peter ever thought to get dinner for her for the hell of it. To let her know he was thinking about her or was worried about her. Yet, a guy who was battling a bad bullet wound infection had done just that.

She swiped the tears away from her eyes and placed a hand over her belly. "Your dad is a good guy. I vow right now, that no matter what happens, you will know how wonderful he is."

Now that she was divorced, she never expected to fall pregnant at all. Seemed fate had other ideas and luckily for her, so far the guy seemed a to be a good one. Although she'd thought that about Peter and look how that had turned out.

One nice gesture didn't mean anything. No matter how much she hoped it did. For the sake of herself and her baby, Suzie needed to remain cautious around Ryan. Jumping in with eyes closed wasn't an option this time. It wasn't just her she had to think about.

Once Ryan was out of hospital, they could talk about making arrangements for how they would handle the pregnancy. But one thing was for certain, no way was she going to let him push her around. When it came to her and her baby, she was the one in charge. Not the sexy, alpha SEAL.

CHAPTER FOUR

A sharp knock was the only warning Ryan had before the door was opened. He looked up and hoped it was the doctor coming to discharge him. God, how he hated lying around like a sack of potatoes. The longer he was laid up the more his conditioning went down.

It had been two days since he'd woken and found Suzie by his bedside. He'd only seen her once since then, when she'd come to see him to thank him for ordering her dinner. Every time a nurse walked in he hoped it would be her. And every damn time, disappointment sliced through him when he was met with an unfamiliar face.

The happy smiles on the nurses' faces dimmed when he scowled at them. He shouldn't take his rotten mood and disappointment that they weren't Suzie out on them. It wasn't their fault.

"I understand you've been giving my nurses a

hard time?" The doctor said as he wandered into the room.

"Not intentionally," he muttered, wondering what sort of reputation he'd garnered around the place over the last couple of days.

"You're just not used to being in a bed all day."

At least the doc understood him. "Pretty much."

"I've got some good news. The infection has cleared up significantly since we've been pumping antibiotics through your IV. I think we can take that out and you can start on a course of tablets."

"So, I can get out today."

The doctor shook his head. "Probably tomorrow, I want to make sure, once we remove the IV, there aren't any flare ups."

Ryan bit back a curse. He hadn't seen any of his team since he'd ended back up in hospital, which could only mean one thing. They'd gone wheels up without him. He fucking hated that he'd let his team down. First by getting shot and then by letting the wound get infected. "Tomorrow for sure I can get out of here?"

The doctor was making notes on the tablet in his hand. "Mmhmmm."

He supposed that was a yes. "Great."

He studied the screen then looked back at Ryan. "I'll get a nurse to come in and remove the drip. You'll be a little more mobile, but I wouldn't do too much, you don't want to aggravate the wound and prolong your stay."

"How long until I'm able to get back into my full training regime?"

The doctor tapped his finger against his lip. "I'd say a month to six weeks."

Disbelief pooled in his stomach. He couldn't be out for that long. "Bullshit."

"Sorry, but you had a serious injury. You need to let your body recover otherwise you could end up taking even longer to get back on track."

The temptation to argue the point with the doctor coalesced inside him. There would be no point arguing with the medical professional. He had no idea what it took to be a SEAL. How they learned to push through the pain. Hell, they had to just to get through BUD/S.

"Right," Ryan responded.

The doctor canted his head to the side and squinted at him, as though trying to determine exactly what was going through Ryan's mind. The guy worked in a military hospital. He should know that what he wanted a patient to do and what the patient did were two entirely different scenarios. He shrugged knowing that no matter what he said, Ryan was planning to do the opposite. "A nurse will be in shortly. I'll see you tomorrow, Mr. Smith."

Ryan slumped against the pillows when the door clicked shut. He rubbed a hand across his eyes, wishing he could turn the clock back and weave right instead of left and the bullet that lodged itself in his leg had whizzed past him and Cowboy and lodged into a tree or something else.

The problem with that particular scenario was he never would've seen Suzie again and found out he was going to be a father.

A father.

Fuck, he hadn't allowed himself to think too long on the bomb she'd dropped on him. He thought back to their one night together. It had been after they'd rescued Italy's girl, Erin and her best friend Antonia from the clutches of Erin's psycho ex. He'd flirted with Suzie at the hospital. Her smile had drawn him in and she'd laughed at his corny jokes. He'd been surprised as hell when she'd accepted his dinner invitation. He'd expected her to turn him down flat. He certainly hadn't expected the flare of desire that punched him in the gut when she'd turned up at the bar dressed in skinny jeans that hugged her legs and ass and a silky blouse that hinted at a nice cleavage. Dinner had led to kisses and tangled sheets.

Ryan's body hardened in response, and he could camp under the tenting in his sheet. It had been a wild night and one he'd remembered on more occasions than he liked to admit.

What he should've done was contacted her again, after he'd woken to find her gone from the hotel room they'd both agreed to finish the night in. Only he'd held back, and he still didn't know what had prevented him from picking up the phone and calling the hospital. Hell, he could've gone and seen her the time he'd visited Erin and Antonia while they'd recovered from their injuries.

Now, here he was in the hospital she worked in

and he hadn't been able to see her. His movement had been limited to dragging the IV pole to the bathroom so he could relieve himself. No way was he going to piss in any bottle and have a nurse carry it to the bathroom. He was a SEAL for fuck sake.

The door opened again, and a nurse bustled through carrying a tray. Damn, still wasn't Suzie.

"Okay Mr. Smith, let's get this IV out of you and then you can have a little freedom."

Freedom.

Yes, the first thing he planned to do is take a walk around and see if he could find Suzie. It was as plain as the fresh scar on his leg Suzie Waterson was avoiding him. The time for avoidance was over. They had things to discuss. Now he knew he was going to be a father, he planned to be involved as much as he could. And he wasn't going to take no for an answer.

The sun beat down on Ryan's face as he sat on a bench in the rose garden at the back of the hospital. It had been two hours since he'd been freed from the confines of clear plastic tubes and the metal stand he'd been attached to.

Two frustrating hours of wandering around looking for Suzie and not finding her. He supposed he could've asked at one of the many nurses stations he'd wandered past, but instinct screamed at him that the last thing Suzie would want was her colleagues asking her why a patient was asking after her.

Had she told anyone she was pregnant? From his calculations, and he was no Einstein when it came to babies, but he checked the calendar and worked out it was almost three months since they'd slept together. He imagined she'd start to show soon and she'd have to answer questions then.

Was she ashamed at being pregnant?

Of course she could be, you doofus. She's going to be a single mom. It maybe the twenty-first century but there were still plenty of people who look down on single moms.

Okay so she may not be ashamed of her situation, but she could be worried about what people would think. Especially since it was fairly obvious she wasn't in a long-term relationship.

Did he want a relationship with Suzie? Apart from the whole being the father of her child thing. Did he want to pursue getting to know her more?

Yes.

For too long he'd been putting off getting in touch with her. He'd talked himself out of it—for reasons he'd yet to work out. But under the sun and in the fresh air, he could admit to himself that when he'd woken alone that morning after, a sense of loss had flowed through him. He'd ignored the sensation. He'd had one night stands before. Usually they were from girls whose mission in life had been to bed a Navy SEAL. On some occasions he'd obliged them. On other's he'd gently rebuffed them.

But with Suzie, their whole interaction had been different. They'd actually talked about things when they'd eaten dinner. It hadn't been meaningless conversations. They'd talked about how she'd got into nursing. He hadn't gone too deep into his career but he'd shared with her the drive he'd had ever since a Navy Veteran had visited his high school on Veteran's Day when he'd been a freshman and talked about the military and the honor he had in representing his country.

It was after that visit that he'd gone home and told his parents he was going to enlist. His parents had cried, both proud and scared for him. Whenever he'd caught his mom looking at him, he always wondered if she was hoping he'd come out and say he'd changed his mind. He'd been one of the dorky kids in high school. The one that was always picked on. He'd been quite familiar with the inside of a toilet bowl, until he started cracking jokes.

Life had become different and he'd been able to tolerate going to classes every day. Graduation hadn't come soon enough and he'd found his place in the military. He'd missed his high school reunions because he'd been deployed. He hadn't made an effort to keep in touch with the guys and they hadn't bother to look him up either.

He still hadn't called his parents to let them know he'd been shot. Mom would pitch a fit, and Dad would have to spend three days calming her down and stopping her from jumping on a plane to come see him. If Ryan had had an extended break from any missions, he should probably see if he could get some time off and make a quick visit home to Oregon and see them. Better to tell her face to face that he'd been hurt than over the phone. At least she'd be able to see for herself that he was okay. It would also give him the opportunity to share the news they were about to become grandparents.

"Hey, Joker, you're a hard man to find."

Ryan looked and saw Cowboy and Red striding toward him. He sat up straighter. "Hey, thought you guys must've been wheels up, since no one came and saw me."

Really, I sound like a whiny ass girl whose best friend hasn't called her for three days. I'm a fucking SEAL.

"Yeah, we were for a couple days. Got back this morning," Red said as he sat down next him. "Why you hangin' out in a garden?"

Ryan itched to ask the guys where they'd been, but he also didn't want to know. He didn't want to think that he could be easily replaced. "Gained my freedom from the IV. You guys here to spring me?"

"Nah, we like the guy who joined us on the recent mission more." Cowboy winked and punched him lightly on the arm. Ryan flinched, not from Cowboy's punch, it wouldn't hurt a flea, but from the confirmation that he could be easily replaced. He'd worked too damn hard to let a bullet wound get him down.

"Yeah, well don't fall in love with him, Cowboy, I'll be back before you know it. And don't forget, I've been on the team longer than either one of you. If anyone's getting replaced it will be one of you two."

"When do you think you'll be back?" Red asked.

That was the million-dollar question, and he had no fucking idea. His leg had hurt like a bitch when he'd been searching for Suzie, another reason why he was sitting on the bench. It amazed him how much conditioning he'd lost in just a couple of weeks of not doing his regular morning PT workouts with the guys.

If his doctor suggested he needed to do any type of physical therapy he'd tell him where he could stick it. In the military, their morning workouts were all the therapy he needed to get himself back on his feet.

"I'm hoping to get out of here in the next day or two and then be back on base the day after."

"You sure that's a good idea?" Cowboy asked. "You had surgery and now an infection. You should make sure you recover properly."

"I'll recover more quickly if I'm back into my regular routine."

"Well, you should listen to the doc—"

"Shut the fuck up, Cowboy," Ryan interjected.

The other man held his arms up in surrender. "Fine, don't be bitching to me when you can't get over a wall. I won't help your sorry ass."

Ryan scrubbed a hand down his face. Shit, now they really were sounding like a group of teenage girls. He shouldn't let his insecurities color his interaction with his team. He wasn't the first guy to get hurt and have to take some time to recover, he won't be the last. "Sorry, I'm just fucking annoyed at being stuck here while you guys are off doing good stuff."

Red chuckled. "Trust me, you're not missing much. This last mission was an escort-the-senators-daughter-to-college gig. Nothing to get too excited about."

"Why the fuck did you guys get that deal?" Ryan asked, kind of glad he had been laid up in hospital.

"Dumb ass luck, I guess," Cowboy responded. "She wasn't even that good looking."

Ryan laughed, his earlier foul mood slowly evaporating. "Sounds like I dodged a bullet."

The two men groaned at his lame ass comment. "That's one thing I haven't missed," Red said. "Your lame jokes."

"Hot nurse alert, ten o'clock." Cowboy hissed out of the corner of his mouth.

It took all of five seconds for Ryan to recognize who Cowboy was referring to. "Keep your dick in your pants. She's off limits."

"What?" Red looked at him as if he'd sprouted another head.

Fuck, I should've kept my mouth shut.

"Ryan, here you are. Dr. Morton thought you'd done a runner. He sent a couple of us looking for you."

Yeah, he could tell how thrilled she was to have been tasked with looking for him. She'd spent the last few days avoiding him.

"Well, you found me, and as you can see I'm fine." His words came out harsher than he intended.

"Right," Suzie crossed her arms over her chest, crushing the lightweight material of her scrub top. His dick twitched at the generous swell of her breasts. "You need to get yourself back in your room, now, preferably."

The guys snorted beside him, clearly enjoying

seeing him get told off. They both stood. Yeah, they weren't going to save his ass, they were itching to get back to base to tell the rest of the guys he was getting his butt whipped by a nurse.

"We were just leaving, ma'am," Cowboy drawled, laying on a thick Texan accent, as if that would make Suzie swoon at his feet. But damn if a light pink hue didn't crawl up her neck and bloom on her cheeks.

He glared at Cowboy, who winked at him. "Later, Joker," he said and if he was wearing hat, Ryan would lay a hundred dollar bet that he'd tip it at Suzie as he walked past her.

"We need you back on the team, Joker," Red informed him before he walked away, smiling at Suzie.

Oh man, without a doubt those two would be itching to get back to the other guys to relay what had just gone down in the hospital's garden.

Silence stretched between him and Suzie. He'd half expected her to follow the guys back to the hospital, not hang around with him. Was she waiting for him to go back to his room?

Ryan studied her a bit closer, noticing the tension lines bracketing her mouth and the furrow between her brow. He stood and walked closer to her. "Are you okay?" he asked softly and reached out to smooth the imperfection between her eyes. Suzie's eyes drifted shut and she swayed a little. He hooked an arm around her and pulled her up against him.

A million sensations flowed through, prickling his skin. He breathed in the light flowery scent of her perfume. It would be so easy to lift her chin and kiss her. It had been too long since he'd been this close to a woman. Ironically, the last woman had been Suzie.

"We shouldn't be doing this," she murmured and pulled away from him. He wanted to pull her close to him again, but he refrained when confusion clouded her blue eyes, giving them a stormy sea look.

"You're right, I'm sorry." He smoothed his hands down the sweatpants he wore. "I suppose I'd better get back to my room."

"Yeah."

Ryan hesitated, waiting to see if she would walk with him, but when her feet remained rooted to the spot he began to move.

"Wait," Suzie called. She caught up to him, which wasn't far as he'd only taken about five steps. "I wanted to ask you something."

"You can ask me anything."

Her mouth opened and then closed, as though she was trying to form the words but finding it difficult to do. "I've got a doctor's appointment in a couple of days. I wanted to know if you wanted to come."

Whatever he'd been expecting Suzie to ask, inviting him to her doctor's appointment was the last thing he ever thought she'd say. "Yes, I'd love to."

Damn, the words exploded out of him like cannon. He didn't want to sound too eager, but this was huge. She was opening up her world to him and he planned to grasp it with two hands.

However, they'd got themselves into this situation, he planned on being by Suzie's side as much as she'd let him. Their child deserved to have two parents who could get along. Who liked each other. And he liked Suzie, in fact, he wanted to get to know her more. Wanted to explore the possibility of seeing if they had a future together. Hell, some marriages started with less than what they had. The big question was, is this something Suzie wanted to pursue or did she want him to be a once a month kind of dad.

CHAPTER FIVE

If the receptionist gave Ryan one more side-eye glance, Suzie was going to march over there and scratch her eyes out. He was hers, not the other girl's.

Whoa, settle down there. Ryan is not your man. He just happens to be the person who donated the necessary ingredient to make a baby.

Suzie closed her thoughts off. What the hell had she been thinking asking him to come to her appointment? Clearly sensible thought had left her when she found him sitting in the hospital's rose garden with two of his work colleagues. If the girl behind the counter wanted to find herself a military man, Suzie would be more than happy to set her up with any one of the soldiers she saw on a regular basis. Anyone, except the man sitting next to her.

Oh God, she needed to get a grip. There was nothing happening between her and Ryan.

Although you'd like there to be.

There was that voice again, telling her what she didn't want to hear, even if there was an ounce of truth to it.

"Miss Waterson?"

Suzie stood at hearing her name, Ryan jumped up and winced as the movement jolted his injured leg. He'd been released from the hospital this morning and Suzie thought he probably could've done with another day of bedrest, but then he wouldn't be able to be here with her. Maybe that would've been a better idea.

No, she wanted Ryan here. Now that the father of her baby was aware he was going to be a dad, she wanted him to be involved. It was apparent from the way he quickly answered her that he wanted to be a part of the process. There were many things they needed to discuss and perhaps, after her appointment, they could get something to eat and sort out some of the logistics of the situation they now found themselves in.

"Are you okay," she asked him as they followed the nurse to the examination room.

"I'm fine. Keep forgetting that quick movements aren't the best idea."

"It will get better."

He grunted a response.

"Miss Waterson, if you'd like to change into this and get up on the bed, the doctor will be with you shortly." She handed Suzie a paper gown. "Sir, if you'd like to wait out here. Miss Waterson will let you know when you can enter the room."

Suzie chuckled at the surprised look on Ryan's face. Clearly, this nurse wasn't swayed by a good looking guy. "I won't be a minute," she told Ryan as she closed the door.

She stripped quickly and donned the gown. "You can come in now," she called out.

"Man, felt like I'd been called to the Commander's office and was about to get roasted."

"Do you get sent to the Commander's office much?" Suzie settled herself on the bed, pulling the paper blanket up over her legs. There really was no point in warming her legs, they were only going to get cold the second she put them in the metal stirrups.

"Nah, not anymore."

"But you used to?"

His lips quirked into a sexy smile, one that melted her insides. Great, the doctor was going to come in and know she was turned on by the man sitting in the chair next to her.

"In the early days I did things I shouldn't have. I learned pretty quickly that guidelines and instructors are there for a reason."

"They usually are," she responded drily.

There was a brisk knock on the door, before it was opened and Suzie's doctor poked her head around the wood. "Hi there, Suzie, all set?" Dr Jones asked.

Suzie nodded and the woman walked in, pausing when she spied Ryan beside her. "Hi, Dr. Jones, this is Ryan Smith and yes he's the father of the baby."

Dr. Jones didn't miss a beat and strode over to Ryan holding her hand out. "Pleasure to meet you, Mr. Smith."

"You as well," Ryan stated.

"Okay then, let's get started. How have you been feeling, Suzie?" Dr. Jones asked as she sat at the small desk in the room.

"Not too bad. The nausea has settled and I'm not as tired."

"Good. You're," she glanced at the computer screen. "Coming up to thirteen weeks, so you're entering your second trimester. You should start feeling a little more energized now."

The doctor asked a few more questions and Suzie was aware of Ryan's hand creeping ever so closer to where hers lay by her side.

"You ready to see this baby of yours?" The doctor asked.

"What?" Ryan's hand closed the minuscule distance and gripped hers.

"I'm having an ultrasound today," Suzie said quietly. It was one of the reasons she asked Ryan to come to the appointment.

"Is that dangerous for you and the baby?" he directed his question at her and not the doctor. It was oddly comforting to think he trusted her over a more qualified doctor.

Suzie squeezed his hand. "It's totally fine. There's no danger to either of us."

"I suppose that was a really stupid question, considering the things I do and the fact that ultrasound is used in physical therapy sessions." A light bloom of red slashed across his cheeks.

She smiled at him and held his gaze. "No, not stupid at all."

They stared at each other for a few moments. The gold flecks in his hazel eyes stood out more than usual. Then again, this was the first time she'd really looked deeply into Ryan's face. Her heart fluttered at the intensity he directed at her.

The sound of a throat clearing finally registered into her consciousness. Suzie dragged her gaze from Ryan and looked at her doctor. The woman wasn't hiding her indulgent smile. "It's always good to see two committed parents."

Looks could be deceiving. At the moment, she and Ryan were anything but committed parents, they were still finding their way around the situation they were in. As if he could tell she was feeling out of sorts with the doctor's comments, Ryan faced the doctor. "More like a nervous dad, here. Mom is in total control of herself."

The doctor chuckled and grabbed a tube of gel. "Okay then, let's get started."

Excitement mingled with nerves as Dr. Jones, lifted her gown to smear the gel on her belly. She started as the coolness of the liquid against her heated flesh.

"Right, what we're going to do is take some measurements to check the progress of the baby's growth," she explained as she moved the wand over her stomach. Suzie's eyes were fixed on the screen as the baby's form materialized.

"That's our baby?" whispered Ryan, awe in every syllable.

Tears filled her eyes. "Yes."

The doctor took the various measurements, but whatever she said to her and Ryan was white noise. Her focus was divided between the images on the screen and the man holding her hand in both of his.

"How about we listen to your baby's heartbeat?" The doctor flicked a couple of switches.

Swoosh! Swoosh! Swoosh!

Echoed around the room, the sound reassuring to her ears.

"That's amazing and so fast. Is that normal?" asked Ryan.

"Perfectly normal, your baby is healthy and strong. Now let's get a good look at your baby's face."

Dr. Turner worked her magic and in the next instant the image on the screen coalesced into a fully formed face, with two closed eyes, a perfect little button nose and rosebud lips.

Suzie had heard about 3D scans but seeing it in action was amazing.

"The next time we do a scan, we should be able to confirm the baby's gender," said Dr. Turner. "That is if you want to find out."

Prior to informing Ryan about his duties as a father, Suzie had determined that she wanted to find out what she was having. She wanted to be able to plan the nursery and start to build up the baby's wardrobe. Now, Ryan had as much right as her to make the decision.

"That's up to Suzie," Ryan stated. "I'm following her lead here."

"Really?" He couldn't mean that, could he?

"Yeah, if you want to find out then I'm totally on board with that. If you don't then I'm okay with that too."

"We've got a few weeks before you have to make that decision. You don't need to let me know now, I was just letting you know you have that option at your next scan." She pressed another couple of buttons on the machine and a soft whirring filled the room. "I've just printed out some pictures for the both of you."

A few moments later she handed the papers to Suzie and another set to Ryan. He had to relinquish his hold on her hand and she wanted to snatch it back immediately. Instead she looked at the pictures. An unbelievable sense of rightness filled her at the images in her hand.

"This is fucking amazing," Ryan said.

Dr. Jones chuckled. "Yes, it is. I'll leave you both now. Don't forget to make your next appointment, Suzie. It was good to meet you too, Ryan."

Suzie bit her lip to hold back her burst of laughter at Ryan's distracted response to Dr. Jones.

The second the door clicked close Ryan stood and framed her face with his hands. "Thank you," he said before he leaned in and captured her lips with his.

Thank goodness she was already laying down because if she'd been standing it was entirely plausible she would currently be a puddle of liquid on the ground. She'd forgotten what it was like to be kissed by Ryan. Forgotten how his aura enveloped her and made her forget her own name. No wonder she fell pregnant, even with wearing protection. Ryan was impossible to resist. Why she hadn't been able to say no to him the night they went out for dinner and ended up in bed.

"Oh sorry, I'll come back in a minute."

Suzie pulled her lips away in time to see the door to the room being closed again. "Oh, geez," she muttered.

Ryan brushed a hand down her cheek and she lifted her eyes to meet his again. "We have a lot to talk about, don't we?"

She could only nod. They did have a ton to talk about. Only she wasn't sure she was ready to face up to it all.

Ryan sat in his car out the front of the complex Suzie lived in, the picture of his child in his hand. He'd lost hours gazing at the picture over the last couple of days. This meeting with Suzie had been eating away at him. He'd wanted to talk to her directly after her doctor's appointment, but she had to go to work. He could've pushed her. He'd already pushed her by kissing her without even asking. It had seemed the most natural thing to do. He'd enjoyed every second of their lip lock.

Now, here he sat, like a nervous teenager wondering if his date's dad was going to eat him alive when he knocked on the door. The likelihood of that happening when he knocked on Suzie's door was slim, but he also couldn't be too sure of her reaction to him, even though it was her idea to meet at her place.

Popping the picture carefully back into his wallet he got out of the car. His movements were becoming looser and looser with each day that passed. He'd even gone to work that day in an attempt to keep his mind off his upcoming meeting with Suzie. The guys had given him a hard time at his distraction, but he managed to fob them off with excuses about taking it easy on his leg. Which was such a lie, a SEAL never took things easy, and the guys knew it, but they kept their opinions to themselves. Although he had to distract Cowboy and Red from asking him all about Suzie seeing as they'd seen her when they visited him at the hospital.

The building Suzie lived in had no doorman or buzzer system to let her know when she had a visitor. He didn't like it at all. The lack of security made his skin crawl. Anyone could enter the building and accost the residents. It didn't matter that the building appeared to be nice and clean and was in a relatively safe area. None of that truly mattered. In his time overseas, he'd seen that even the nicest looking person could be hiding a semi-automatic beneath their jacket.

He took a couple of seconds to let the worry drain out of him. The worst thing he could do was storm up to Suzie's floor and tell her she needed to move to a safer building. Regardless of the fact that they were going to be parents, he didn't have a right to lecture her about her living arrangements. He also had a gut feeling she wouldn't appreciate his demands. She may look tough, but he'd seen the hint of vulnerability within her, even though she tried hard to hide it.

Once he determined he was in control of his emotions and wouldn't go all heavy-handed Navy SEAL on her, he strode to the small lobby that housed the elevators.

Thanks to Tex and his skills, he knew Suzie lived on the third floor. That was how he'd been able to get food delivered to her after he'd seen her in the hospital. The ex-SEAL hadn't asked questions, well not too many, when he'd phoned him asking for the information. Tex had helped Italy and a former teammate Ash with their fiancée's, so the former SEAL turned computer whiz didn't seem to have a problem getting Ryan the information he needed as well.

The elevator arrived and he stepped in, pressing the required disc. The cart cranked into motion. While the building looked modern, it appeared the elevator was older than time itself, or the motor was about to clap out. If it did he hoped he wasn't anywhere near it and neither was Suzie.

On the third floor, he got his bearings, noting where the exits were located if, for some reason, he and Suzie had to make an escape. Not that it was likely, but his training was ingrained.

He'd almost reached her home, when a door at

the end of the hallway cracked open. A head popped out and Ryan took note of the owner. He wore thin wire-rimmed round glasses, that belonged back in the nineties. His hair was slicked over to the left and he couldn't tell if his hair was a dark color naturally or because of all the product in it was making it look dark. Immediately the hairs on the back of Ryan's neck stood to attention when he closed the door again. Ryan didn't like the vibe the guy was putting out. His examination of Ryan wasn't that of a curious neighbor. It had an almost sinister quality, which was stupid, but experience had told him to trust his gut, and his gut was screaming that Suzie's neighbor wasn't the type of person he could trust. He would have to ask her about him.

Ryan made a mental note to get Tex to see if there was any information on the guy who lived in the apartment four doors down from Suzie. When he left, he'd find out the exact number. If they guy was hiding something, Tex would find it and then Ryan would do whatever it took to keep Suzie and their child safe.

Happy he had a solid plan in place, he rapped his knuckles against her door, nerves slamming into him with the force of one of his brothers tackling him to the ground to avoid flying bullets.

The door opened and he lost the ability to speak. Dressed in tight fighting jeans and a fluffy cream sweater that accentuated her breasts he fought down the temptation to pull her in his arms and continue on where they left off in the doctor's office, only this time going all the way until he was balls deep inside her.

He gave himself a mental shake. This wasn't what he'd come here to do. There was every chance, even though Suzie had returned his kiss, the last thing she wanted was to end up in bed with him. The one and only time they had, ended with them becoming parents. Strangers to parents in the space of one night.

"Are you planning on coming in or even saying something?"

His mind registered her words, but a movement out of the corner of his eye drew his attention from her. The guy from the down the hall now had half his body out his door and was watching Ryan avidly.

"Something I can help you with?" he asked, directing a don't-mess-with-me look down the hall.

He darted back into his apartment, ignoring Ryan's question. The protective instinct, which had fired into overdrive the second he found out Suzie was pregnant, pushed him into action and he strode into Suzie's place. He wrapped an arm around her and ushered her down the small hallway into her living room.

"Who's the dude who lives four doors down from you?" he demanded.

Suzie stepped away from him and planted her hands on her hips. "Excuse me?"

"I think you heard me."

He really should've been paying attention to her posture. It would've given him a good idea of what she was about to do next. "Ow." Ryan rubbed the spot on his chest where her finger jabbed him. "What was that for?"

"You don't get to come into my home and start spouting off demands. I'm not one of your teammates."

"Babe, I don't hand out demands on my team. I follow them." He winked hoping to bring a smile to her face. If anything, the way her eyebrows drew closer together it had the opposite effect of what he had been trying to achieve.

"God, if it wasn't for the fact that we really need to talk about the baby and what we're going to do. I'd kick you out so fast you wouldn't know what hit you."

He may go through life making jokes, but he wasn't completely insensitive. His demands about her neighbor had triggered a response in Suzie and, if he wanted to have any chance in salvaging the evening, he needed to take evasive actions.

Ryan rolled his shoulders to lessen the tension that had been riding him since he'd seen the asshole's face poking out of his apartment. He took a tentative step toward her. When she didn't back away he closed the distance and reached out and took hold of her hand, rubbing his thumb over the top of her palm. "I'm sorry, Suzie."

CHAPTER SIX

Why did he have to be so sweet?

The unbidden thought drained away the rest of her anger. She wanted to grasp it back, cloak herself in it. Anger was much better to deal with than the wave of lust and need that had swamped her when she'd opened the door to him.

She so didn't need to feel this constant attraction to the guy. It would only lead her into trouble. Trouble she'd got a glimpse of when he'd marched her into her own home and demanded she answer his question.

If they were to have any chance of a future, for their child's sake not for her, then she needed to lay some ground rules.

She extracted her hand from his hold and clasped them together, savoring the lingering warmth from his touch. "I accept your apology, but we need to get something straight. In my personal life, I don't take orders from anyone. If you want to know something ask me, don't demand."

His eyes narrowed for a fraction of a second and she braced herself for a fight. A *how dare you speak to me that way*. It's exactly what Peter would've done. He would've got in her face and yelled at her.

Ryan, however, did the opposite. He took a step back and nodded. "Fair enough."

"Really? That's all you're going to say? You aren't going to tell me that you will talk to me anyway you want?"

Why was she pushing this? The guy agreed with her. Did she really want to be yelled at the way Peter used to?

No.

She was done with that part of her life and her telling Ryan, challenging him, was her way of keeping in total control.

"Yes,. I respect you, Suzie. What do you want me to do? Argue with you until you see things my way. That's not how I operate."

Sincerity tinged every single word he spoke. He wasn't just saying it to placate her. To snowball her into thinking one thing about him when the opposite was true. The man standing in front of her, the father of her child, was completely different to the man she'd been married to.

In that second, relief flooded her like a warm shower after a cold day. Relief that she hadn't fallen pregnant while married to Peter. They'd tried to have a child over the short period they'd been married, but God or fate had been watching over her. The question was. Why had fate and/or God chosen Ryan to be the father of her child? Why now when she was in charge of her own destiny.

Warm hands framed her face and nudged a little, encouraging her to look up at him. "I promise to be more aware of how I frame my questions in the future. But please, do me a favor and answer this one. Do you know the guy who lives a couple of doors down from you?"

In the grand scheme of things, his initial question wasn't an intrusive one. Her reaction had been a tad over the top. At least, though, they'd reached an understanding. And she had no doubt Ryan wouldn't go back on his word, like Peter had done time and time again. Ryan honored the code of the Navy SEALs, the brotherhood, he would honor her. Now she could answer his question. "I think you're talking about Jeffery?"

Ryan released his hold on her face and grabbed for one of her hands. She liked the connection between them. "Tall, thin, slicked back hair, wire rimmed glasses dude."

"Yes, that's Jeffery. What about him?"

"How well do you know him?" he asked as he led her to her couch and sat down, bringing her with him. Their bodies bumped and a delicious thread of warmth wove its way through her. She scooted back to put a little distance between them. No way would she be able to form coherent words sitting so close to him, but he squeezed her hand, indicating the last thing he wanted was for her to move away from him.

It took her a moment to relax with being so close to Ryan and gather her thoughts and think about his question. "I can't say I really know him that well. He says hello and sometimes we chat about our days. Normal stuff neighbors would talk about."

The last thing she planned on telling Ryan was how Jeffery had seemed to be a little more stalkerish of late. Always appearing when she left for work or when she arrived home.

Like a lightbulb going off over the head of a character in a cartoon, she recalled what Ryan said before he walked into her home. "That's who you were talking to after I opened the door, wasn't it?"

"I wouldn't say *talking to* in the strictest sense of the phrase. I'm not sure I trust him. He has a look about him."

The fact Ryan had honed in on Jeffery shouldn't have surprised her. In his job, the ability to judge and read people in seconds was the difference between life and death for military guys and more particularly SEALs.

Should she tell him what she was feeling about Jeffery? Without a doubt if she voiced her concerns Ryan would come all over protective and want to control her movements and actions. While that was comforting, it went against everything she'd strived to achieve since she walked out on Peter. Her ex had dominated every aspect of her life, except the bedroom. In the bedroom he was lackluster and she hadn't realized how mediocre their sex life had been until the one night she'd spent with Ryan. That night she'd found out what a good sex life should be.

"If you're thinking this hard and long about what I said, then you must have some concerns about him."

Damn.

"Okay, don't make me regret saying anything you." She eyeballed him, hoping to get her point across that when it came to her life, she steered the ship.

"In addition to my other promise, I promise to make you not regret saying anything to me."

He smiled in a boyish *trust me* way and she steeled herself to stop from melting into a heap. "Over the last couple of weeks he's been a bit more attentive than I'm comfortable with."

Being so close to him she felt every muscle in his body tightening until they were almost as hard as a rock. She was also aware of the way he took in some deep breaths, encouraging those tight muscles to loosen. "How long has he been living in the building?"

Not the question she'd been expecting, but okay. "He was here when I moved in a year ago."

Ryan opened his mouth and then closed it. She knew he wanted to interrogate her about Jeffery, but he was controlling the urge. Instead he nodded as if coming to a silent agreement within himself. "Okay."

"You want to ask more questions, I can see it."

"Doesn't matter what I want. Besides we aren't here to talk about your neighbor. We're here to talk about us and," he paused and laid his hand on her belly. "Our baby."

The thread of warmth that had been traveling through her burst into flame. How could he do this to her? How could one touch set her alight as though she'd never been touched by a man before? It was insane and ridiculous. Yet it felt right. As though everything in her life had been leading up to this moment.

In the back of her mind a little voice was cautioning her that he'd given up on finding out about Jeffery too easily. But it was drowned out by the other voice encouraging her to lean in to his touch. To close the gap and kiss him. Like the kiss they'd shared in the doctor's surgery. The same kiss that had been playing on repeat in her mind ever since they parted ways. It was surprising she hadn't stuck herself with an IV needle on her shift, she'd been that distracted.

"God, you're so beautiful," he whispered, bringing her back from the deep recesses of her mind. She registered his lips were a hairs-breadth away from hers.

Had she voiced her need to him? One glance at the slumberous look in his eyes and she had her answer–he wanted to kiss her as much as she wanted to kiss him. The problem was, why wasn't he taking the final step. He hadn't hesitated at her appointment. He'd taken.

"Can I kiss you?" The question shocked and delighted her. Never before had anyone asked to kiss her. Not even the night they slept together. The passion between them had flared to life the second she'd arrived at the restaurant. It was why they ended up in a nearby hotel and not at her place or his. The thought of having to travel any distance had been abhorrent to them. It had been freeing to do something so out of character for her. Following an attraction she'd never experienced before.

"Yes."

He groaned, and his lips met hers. For a second they merely touched, as if they were kissing for the first time. A sweet kiss. A kiss that promised heaven if she wanted to reach for it again. Boy, did she want to reach for it again. She placed her hands on his shoulders and moved until she was straddling his legs, their crotches meeting. His hands gripped her waist, preventing her from moving. Like she had any plans to move from this position.

Ryan's hands slip up her back, taking her sweater with them. The cool air caressed her exposed skin. His fingers traced up and down her spine, her skin tingling. Suzie wanted to get her hands on him. Reacquaint herself with the ridges of his hard chest. Kiss all his scars. Relive the sensation of him sliding into her, pausing before he moved in a steady pace in and out of her. Her hips mimicked the road her thoughts were heading down. Her panties dampened as she rubbed herself along his hard length protruding through the denim of his jeans.

A moan of disappointment escaped her when he dragged his lips away and pushed her back so their bodies weren't so tightly locked together.

"As much as I want to take this further. I really do think we need to stop and talk."

How the hell could the man think clearly when all she could think about was getting him naked? Shouldn't it have been her that put the brakes on? Guys normally thought with their dicks and women thought with their hearts. Yet role reversal at its finest was occurring between them.

As much as she longed to continue what they were doing, her voice of reason wrestled control back. Ryan was right, they needed to talk. Plus, she had promised him dinner and she needed to check on it.

Reluctantly she wiggled back along his legs until her feet touched the ground. She pulled her sweater down as she stood.

"You're right, and I need to check dinner. Why don't you come into the kitchen?"

"Give me a minute and I'll be there," he said ruefully as he lifted his butt and adjusted his jeans. His arousal was as plain as the nose on her face. Poor guy had to feel uncomfortable. "Shit, Suzie, keep looking at me that way and I'll forget about being a gentleman and take you right here on the couch."

Her blood sizzled in delight as images of her and Ryan on the couch pummeled her brain. "Not the worst of ideas," she murmured. He groaned, and she decided to take pity on him. "Kitchen's down the hall. Come find me when you're ready."

"Uh huh."

She shook her head as she walked the short distance from her living room to the kitchen. In all honesty she hoped Ryan took a little time before he joined her. The room wasn't huge, and she had an inkling that his presence would fill the space, tempting her to see if she could persuade him to eat her instead.

Heat swamped her. What the hell was she thinking? This wasn't her. This wasn't how she normally acted. She could try and blame it on pregnancy hormones, she was after all heading into her second trimester and the books she'd been reading had all stated her sexual appetite would return. It wasn't her hormones though. A couple of kisses with Ryan and it seemed her desires had all the subtlety of a herd of elephants.

She moved over to the sink and flicked on the cold water faucet, running her wrists beneath the clear liquid. Her body temperature lowered and when she figured she had her emotions under control she turned it off and dried her hands.

The timer on the oven beeped at the same time and she crossed the tiled floor to pull out the dish of enchiladas she'd made. The aroma of the tangy tomato sauce assaulted her senses and her stomach grumbled.

"Something smells good."

She turned and almost burned Ryan with the hot pan. She was right, he did fill the room, with not only his physical self but the air of self assurance and confidence that surrounded him. "Move or you're going to get burned."

His eyebrow quirked in surprise at her curt tone

but took a couple of steps back. In two steps she was at the small table tucked into the corner of the room and placed the food down.

"Take a seat I'll just get the salad." She went to move past him, but he grabbed hold of her hand. "Yes?"

"Is everything okay?"

"Fine."

"Italy maybe the only guy on the team with a significant other, but even I know when a woman says *fine* she's anything but fine. So, what gives?"

Suzie huffed out a breath. She had no idea why she'd gone from vixen to bitch in thirty seconds. Ryan hadn't done anything wrong when he halted their kisses. She was just so confused with her whole life at the moment. Everything was turning upside down and she didn't know how to control it anymore. She'd fought hard for her independence. To stand on her own two feet and make her own decisions about her life and where it was headed. But right at this moment, all she wanted to do was lay her head on Ryan's strong chest, have his arms wrap around her and take away the decision making from her.

But she couldn't do that. Before Ryan had landed in her hospital she'd made the decision to travel the pregnancy road alone. She'd come to grips with it and had started making plans. Now that was all up in the air because of the man standing in front of her.

"I know the reason I'm here tonight is to talk about the baby and how we're going to move forward, but if it's too much for you I can leave. I won't be offended, even though those enchiladas look even better than the ones I get from my favorite Mexican restaurant." He reached out and stroked a finger down her cheek. "You won't get any pressure from me, Roses. You are in control of this thing between us, not me."

Suzie couldn't help it, she burst into tears.

If there was one thing Ryan didn't know how to deal with, that was crying women. Fortunately, when on a rescue mission and a woman started to cry, Robot was the guy to deal with them. Although on the last mission, the one he tried to block out because he would have to remember how he'd gotten shot, T-Rex had been the one to comfort their hostage.

This was one situation he couldn't walk away from. One he didn't want to. Suzie needed him for emotional support and, even though he didn't have a clue on how to handle it, he would.

"Hey, I'm sorry I didn't mean to make you cry."

She sniffed loudly and very unladylike. He had no doubt under different circumstances she'd be embarrassed with the sounds erupting from her. No way was he going to make her feel bad for being human.

"I'm s-s-sorry." She hiccuped. "I'm not u-u-usually so e-e-emotional."

With one hand holding her tightly against his body, he used his other to hook a finger under her chin and lifted her face so she was looking at him.

Even with tear tracks staining her face, puffy eyes and red nose she was the most beautiful woman he'd ever seen. "Never apologize for being you. I happen to like you exactly the way you are."

Her mouth formed an O as though she couldn't believe his words. Had someone battered her down so much she didn't know her own worth? He could relate to that. All through school he'd been the guy who was the weakest link on every sports team. The pity pick because the school had a policy of if anyone showed interest in sport they would have a turn on the court for basketball or the field for football.

The only place he'd ever felt any sort of value was the second he joined his SEAL team. He'd been relied upon and respected. He wanted to give Suzie that feeling. Wanted her to know he appreciated the person she was.

Their eyes stayed focused on each other for endless moments. It would be so easy to kiss her again. Boy, did he want to do that. He wanted nothing more than to drown in her embrace. He controlled the urge though. The last thing she needed was for him to go all alpha male on her.

"Let's eat," he said, breaking the connection and tamping down the fire threatening to engulf them.

For a moment, he didn't think she was going to move, but she reluctantly inched away from him. He missed the contact, but he needed the distance himself to accept the thought flowing through his mind. A thought he never imagined he would be having.

Suzie Waterson was becoming important to him, and not just because of the child they'd made together. She was becoming important in the way Erin was to Italy. The way Maria was to Ash.

And it scared the hell out of him.

CHAPTER SEVEN

Dinner was over and Ryan had insisted on doing the dishes while she relaxed in the living room. The clattering coming from the kitchen had her wondering if it was such a good idea to readily agree to his suggestion. It didn't sound like any plates were being broken, maybe chipped. Suzie immediately squashed the thought. It wasn't any different to the sounds she made when she did her own washing up. She needed to trust the guy. Hadn't he proven to her this evening that he was the complete opposite of Peter? She needed to stop comparing the two. Stop expecting Ryan to act the same way as Peter. If she'd burst into tears in front her former husband, he'd have told her to quit being a baby. He never would've pulled her into his embrace like Ryan had done.

"I left the dishes where I didn't know where they

went on your table. Do you need a drink or anything?"

Ryan stood in the doorway, all tall and delicious looking in his jeans and grey button-down shirt. There were a couple of wet patches on his top. He looked sexily rumpled and a desire to be wrapped in his strong arms again washed over her.

Insanity.

That was the only word that could describe her visceral reaction to him. She was slowly going insane.

"You do realize I asked you over to dinner. I should be the one offering to get you a drink."

He sauntered into the room and sat down on the couch next to her. "You cooked dinner for me."

"And you cleaned up," she countered. "The least I can do is be the one offering you after dinner refreshments."

A wicked gleam entered his eyes and she had a fair idea which road his mind was headed down. A road she wouldn't mind traveling but not tonight. They still hadn't addressed the reason Ryan was sitting in her apartment. Their child.

He leaned a fraction closer to her. "Please don't tempt me, Ryan," she whispered.

"Tempt you how?"

"By making me forget the reason you're here. For wanting to go back to the night we met and experience what happened in that hotel room all over again."

His eyes darkened with every word she spoke until they were almost black. His breathing was coming as fast as hers. Only a few inches separated their lips. "Would it be so bad?" he asked.

She laid a hand on his thigh, the muscle jumping beneath her touch. Suzie didn't have to look down to see the bulge of his erection against the zipper of his jeans. She could tell his body would be primed for action because her panties were wet with longing.

Her tongue darted out to moisten her dry lips and Ryan groaned closing his eyes. "You are a siren in scrubs, Suzie Waterson."

She laughed at his description. But it had the desired effect and broke the sexual tension clouding them. "Let me tell you, there's nothing remotely attractive about hospital scrubs."

"I don't know. They look pretty sexy on you. It's probably a good thing you didn't visit me too much while I was in hospital. Those gowns you make patients wear are pretty unforgiving when it comes to disguising a man's desire."

"Ugh," she groaned. "That's terrible."

He shrugged his impressive shoulders as if he was an innocent in this sexual banter flying between them. "It's the truth."

"A truth I really didn't want to know, thank you very much. I have to go back to work tomorrow wearing scrubs. I'm never going to be able to look at a male patient again."

"You can't tell me that you don't get a reaction when you give a guy a sponge bath."

Suzie shook her head, but couldn't stop the smile

tugging at her lips. "I cannot believe I am having this conversation with you. You are insane, Ryan Smith."

"I made you smile and that's all worth it."

Damn, here goes that sexual attraction again. She really needed to get a handle on her reaction around him.

Think of the baby. You know the one the two of you created. The one you saw on a grainy black and white screen a few days ago. The reason Ryan is sitting on the couch next to you.

Yes, that little voice in her head sounded very reasonable. "We still need to talk, Ryan. About the baby and," she waved her hand around in the air. "Everything."

Ryan grabbed hold of her hands and held them firmly. "I will do whatever you want me to do. If you only want me to see the baby once a month. I'll do that. If it's only financial involvement then I can do that too. I would like to be a part of this baby's life, but I know this pregnancy wasn't what you planned for your life. I will support you in any way you want me to. As I said earlier, you're in charge here, not me."

He'd given her an out by saying he would only provide financial support. She knew SEAL teams and they went on long missions. Missions where he would be gone for weeks on end where he wouldn't be able to see her or the baby.

Remembering what he did. How dangerous it was should have been all she needed to take him up on the finance only offer. Only she couldn't do that to him.

Or her baby, regardless of that being her original plan when she'd seen the word *Pregnant* show up in the digital screen on the white stick. Ryan was sitting beside her offering his support and it was up to her with how much she gave him.

Taking a deep breath, she squeezed his hands. What she said next could have him running for the hills. It was a risk she was willing to take because her instincts were screaming at her that she would be rewarded greatly. "I believe there is something between us, Ryan. Something more than the baby we created. I want you by my side, every step of the way. But only if you want to."

Ryan leaned forward, touching his forehead to hers. This close it was impossible to read the expression in his face. In his eyes. He could be getting ready to say goodbye. Suzie really hoped that wasn't the case. "I want that very much, Roses. And yes, there is something between us. But with my job and all that it entails, are you ready for it?"

Suzie knew what he was alluding to. It mirrored her thoughts before she told him she wanted to explore this thing growing between them. If she backtracked now she wasn't only hurting herself and her baby, she was hurting Ryan. "Yes." She practically whispered the word. Now that didn't sound convincing. Breaking the connection of the touching foreheads she straightened her shoulders. "Yes, Ryan. I'm ready."

"You won't regret this, I promise."

As he pulled her tightly against him, she hoped

they'd made the right decision. How had one night ended turned her life upside down?

The next day Ryan arrived at PT with a spring in his step and a smile as wide as the ocean fixed on his face. When he'd arrived at Suzie's place the previous evening he never imagined that when he'd left he'd be embarking on a serious relationship with her. The sexual attraction between them couldn't be denied. Hell, they'd breached the latex barrier and created a baby.

He refused to the let the thought form that if he hadn't been shot he may never have seen Suzie again, nor found out he was going to be father.

"Oooooh lookie here, someone got lucky last night," hollered Cowboy.

Ryan rolled his eyes. "Shut up."

"Come on, you can't turn up here skipping down the beach like a little girl with a big smile and expect us to be satisfied with *shut up*," mocked Red.

"I was not skipping."

A hand clapped him on the back. "You kind of were, dude," said Italy.

Shit. Had he really been skipping? No, SEALs don't skip. "Whatever." Ryan shrugged. "I'm in a good mood. What's the crime with that?"

"The crime is," started Robot as he walked to where Ryan stood. "unless you spill your guts, I'm gonna work everyone's ass three times harder than normal."

Groans and grumbles erupted between his teammates.

"Seriously? When did we become teenage girls who shared secrets? Have you guys been braiding each other's hair since I've been off?" He countered.

He supposed he could give them something. Like he'd met a nice girl. No way was he blabbing the news that he was about to be a father. That tidbit he wanted to keep close to his chest. It was still new to him and he wanted to savor the feeling of knowing it was just between him and Suzie. He didn't even know if she'd mentioned to any of her work colleagues that she was pregnant. Did she have a best friend like Antonia was to Erin? There was so much they still had to learn about each other. He was looking forward to finding it all out.

"I know, it's that nurse from the hospital. The one from the garden," Cowboy puffed out as they all started a slow jog down the beach.

Ryan's wound pinched with each stride, but he gritted his teeth and kept going. The only way to get stronger was to work through the pain. That philosophy had gotten him through BUD/S training, it would get him through this.

"It has to be her," Red yelled over his shoulder as he jogged to the front of the group. "He hasn't said a word."

The temptation to roll his eyes again at his teammates antics was strong, but it also made him smile.

To know his band of brothers were interested in his life cemented the friendship they all shared. "Fine. Yes, it's the nurse from the hospital."

They stopped, all of them drawing in deep lungfuls of air. "Hey, when Erin and Antonia were in the hospital, weren't you flirting with a nurse then? Is it her?" asked Italy.

One thing about SEALs they were able to direct their attention to many things all at once. It kept them safe on missions, so he wasn't surprised at Italy's question. His mind may have been full of worry about his girlfriend, but he still paid attention to what was happening around him.

"Yeah, that's her," he responded as he dropped to the sand and started doing pushups.

For the next thirty minutes conversation was kept to a minimum as they went through their training regime. Ryan was glad for the reprieve but knew it would be short lived. One thing he knew about his brothers, once they got onto an interesting topic, they didn't let up until they had all the information. Even if that topic was his relationship.

They arrived back at base and headed for the locker room to shower and change and get ready for the day. Ryan was standing at his locker, towel around his waist when a hand landed on his shoulder. He looked and found Robot standing behind him. "Get together my place this weekend, bring your new girl so we can meet her."

He walked off before Ryan had a chance to open his mouth and protest. What he and Suzie shared was brand new, exposing her to his team could scare her away. He'd seen the hint of fear in her eyes when he'd talked about his job as they discussed if they were going to pursue a relationship. He'd wanted to give her a chance to get used to the idea of dating a Navy SEAL before bringing his team into it. Looks like he wasn't going to get that opportunity. "Sure, I'll see if she's free."

Another thing he needed to find out, what her shifts were. Plus, he needed to contact Tex to see if he could find out information about her neighbor. Perhaps Ryan needed to make himself seen more often around Suzie so the other guy would get the idea she was off the market.

He smiled as he thought about Suzie, wondering if she was working today or if she was at home. How was she feeling? Did she suffer morning sickness? The doctor said she was in her second trimester and she should be feeling better.

"Brother, you've got it bad."

Ryan looked to his left to find Italy standing beside him, grinning like a loon. "What ya talking about, Italy?"

"You're smiling like a little kid on Christmas morning. It only means one thing."

"Yeah, what's that."

"You're falling in love."

Ryan laughed at the notion. A notion he didn't want to look too closely at. How could he possibly be falling in love with Suzie? They'd hardly spent any time together. Sure, they were about to be parents, and the sexual attraction sizzled between them. But it wasn't love. Was it?

"Joker, your face is priceless. Here's where you'd crack a joke, but by the looks of you, you don't want to make one." Italy clapped him on the back and walked away, leaving him to his thoughts.

His teammate was right, the last thing he felt like doing was telling a lame joke. It was what he did when he wanted to take the heat off himself. He'd always used as a way to get people to accept him. It had worked in high school, and when he'd initially enlisted in the Navy. No one thought, geeky Ryan Smith could make it through BUD/S training. He'd proven everyone wrong, but, on occasions, he still didn't feel like he belonged. At the back of his mind was always the thought he could be replaced. Hadn't it been what he'd focused on the whole time he was in hospital with his infection?

A slamming of locker jolted him from his introspection. He needed to get a grip of himself. Inattention could get him, or his teammates hurt or killed. That wasn't going to happen on his watch.

Ever.

Suzie's stomach somersaulted and she took deep breaths. Now that would be an entrance wouldn't it, tossing her cookies the second she stepped into Ryan's team leader's backyard. No wait, team lead, that's the correct term. She'd asked Ryan a ton of questions about his team members when he asked her if she'd like to go to Robot's place. At least she thought they were going to Robot's place. All these nicknames were confusing.

Her step faulted the closer they got to the gate. She could do this. She could.

"You okay, Roses?" Ryan asked.

"Yeah." She really wasn't but she couldn't let Ryan know that.

Ryan tugged her to the side of the gate and pulled her close, his arms entwining loosely around her waist. She shivered in delight at being held so closely. Since dinner at her place, Ryan had been around most nights. They'd kissed more times than she ever had without taking it the next step and having sex. Oh, there was some serious touching involved and he'd brought her to release just by sucking on her breasts, something that she'd never experienced before.

But they hadn't taken it to the next step. Ryan had told her he wanted the next time they slept together to be perfect. Hell, every time they'd made out on the couch had been perfect for her, but her romantic soul found it sweet that he wasn't rushing her into bed. After all they'd already done that. But it was a place she definitely wanted to fall into again.

"If you're feeling at all uncomfortable we'll leave. Just say the word. The guys can be a little over the top on occasion."

She reached up and cupped his cheek, touched by his thoughtfulness. There was so much more to Ryan

'Joker' Smith than she'd ever thought. Did his teammates know this or did he not show it to them? Probably the latter. No way would Ryan want to appear weak in front of his teammates.

Just like she wouldn't. "I'll be fine. Yes, I'm nervous, but I work in a military hospital. You guys aren't the easiest of patients. I can hold my own." Yes, she could and she needed to remember that.

"I'm sure you can. And if I forget to say it later on, I'm really glad you're here with me."

He leaned forward and placed his lips over hers. Her body melted at the contact. Her mouth opened wider to allow his tongue entrance. Her nipples peaked against her bra and desire gathered low between her legs.

Before they could get too carried away, Ryan broke their connection and rested his cheek against hers. A puff of his breath tickling her ear. She went to move away from him. This close she was tempted to drag him back to his car and demand he drive her back to his or her place and forget all about this party.

He halted her progress. "Wait. I want to hold you for a few seconds longer. I know the moment I get in there I'm not going to be able to spend more than five minutes with you."

Suzie laid her head on his chest, she didn't mind him holding her for a little while longer.

"How long have you and Joker been seeing each other?" asked Erin, Italy's fiancée, as she sat down next to her, two glasses of wine in her hand.

"Not long." She took the glass of wine Erin held out and placed it on the table in front of her. Like the other glass she'd been given, Suzie would leave it there when she walked away. Ryan had told her he hadn't mentioned to his team that they were expecting. He said that he would tell them when she was happy for him to mention it. Honestly, she had no problem if wanted to shout it out loud, but she liked that he was waiting for her.

"You meet when Antonia and I were in hospital, right?"

Suzie nodded around the mouthful of food she'd forked into her mouth. She hadn't met Erin or Antonia when they'd been in the hospital, but she had today. Once she swallowed her food she confirmed her nod. "Yeah, we went to dinner that night, but we didn't exchange numbers."

"Dinner was a bust then, huh? Nice of you to give him a second chance."

As much as she tried to control the rush of blood to her face, Suzie couldn't. Erin's eyebrows rose up. "Ohhh," she said and started laughing. "It was like that, was it."

The evidence of their one night was going to be showing soon. SEALs weren't dumb and they'd all work out when exactly she'd fallen pregnant. No point denying what happened that night. It was the best night of her life. One she wanted to experience again. "I'd lie, but there's no point. Yes, we had a one night stand."

"Looks like it's a bit more than that," Erin said quietly.

Immediately Suzie's senses went on high alert. "What do you mean?"

"Well, I'm guessing you saw Joker again after he was shot, seeing as you're a nurse and all. Being the flirt he is, you couldn't resist seeing him again, and here you are."

Relief flowed through Suzie, for a second she was worried that Erin had worked out she was pregnant. "Yeah, something like that."

"A baby does complicate things though, doesn't it?"

Erin made her declaration so casually, Suzie was relieved she hadn't taken another mouthful of food, otherwise she would've spat it out over the table. "Sorry, what did you say?"

Erin leaned closer. "You're pregnant, aren't you."

Again, what was the point in denying the truth. She may have lied to her friends about how controlling Peter had been, but these people standing in the backyard were important to Ryan. She didn't want to be known as a liar. "Yes, but you can't tell anyone."

"Joker doesn't know?" Erin blurted out.

Suzie looked around to see if anyone was watching them, but everyone in the yard where caught up in their own conversations. "Yes, he knows. When I saw him again I told him. I couldn't keep it from him, even though I'd decided to go the solo route. Now that's all changed, which is fine. But how did you know?"

"Takes one to know one." Erin said with a smile.

Hang on a second, was Erin saying she was pregnant too. No, that couldn't be right, she'd brought her a glass of wine when she sat down. Suzie looked at the glassware, noticing there was no indication the glass had been anywhere near Erin's mouth. "I take it no one knows?" she asked and nodded at the wine glass.

"No. I found out yesterday. Even Antonia doesn't know."

Suzie looked over the group of people and found Antonia in a corner talking to Robot. Well, talking was a mild expression, it looked like whatever they were talking about was getting pretty heated. She wondered if they'd been an item and were now no longer one. But it wasn't her business to ask, she was the new girl.

"Congratulations, that's exciting. I'm sure Carlos will be very excited. Ryan was, once he got over the shock."

Erin laughed. "This is totally unplanned, but yeah…" Her voice dropped an octave as she stared directly at her man. "He'll be totally excited."

Suzie smiled when she heard the tenderness in the other woman's voice as she talked about her man. "When do you plan on telling him?"

"Probably tomorrow morning when I'm barfing.

That's the reason I went to the doctor, because I was throwing up so much. Carlos was worried."

"Oh yeah, been there done that, although not every day. It will pass."

Erin grimaced. "That's what my doctor said."

"Guess we need to find a way to dump our wine without anyone being suspicious," Suzie said as she observed Ryan breaking away from the guys he was talking to and heading in her direction. She couldn't help the way her lips spread into a grin as he approached.

"Girl, you've got it bad," whispered Erin under her breath. "Welcome to the club."

Suzie didn't know which club Erin was talking about, but she hoped it was the pregnant club, because any other club was one she didn't want to belong to. That other club meant giving up control of her life and she definitely wasn't going down that route again.

CHAPTER EIGHT

The streetlamp flickered before flaring back to life as Ryan pulled up out front of Suzie's building. He'd had a great time with her at Robot's place. She'd slipped into the group really easily. It had been difficult to keep from stealing kisses from her every chance he got, but he'd controlled himself. He hadn't wanted to embarrass her with an abundance of public displays of affection, and he knew the guys would give him a hard time. Hell, he joined in in giving Italy shit every time he'd grabbed Erin to kiss her.

"Do you want to come up?" Suzie asked quietly as the time they spent in the car stretched out.

"Do you want me to?" Shit, what the fuck was he doing answering her question with a question of his own? He may have only had Suzie back in his life for a short time, but he was well aware she was independent and didn't do anything she didn't want to. If she asked him if he wanted to go to her place, she meant it.

"Wait," he held up his hand when she went to speak. "Yes, Suzie, I'd love to come up."

"Great." She rolled her eyes as she laughed, the light tinkling sound making him smile wider than he already was. He didn't think he'd smiled so much as he had Robot's place. The party had been a lot of fun.

Ryan got out of the car and walked around the front to open the door for Suzie. He wrapped an arm around her waist, holding her close as he closed the door and locked the car.

The street light flickered again.

"The City really needs to do something about that light," he commented as they walked into the building.

"It always flickers, but it never goes out. I think the City has bigger things to worry about than a dodgy lightbulb."

"It's not safe. I don't like it."

Suzie stiffened by his side, the action surprising. "It doesn't matter if you like it or not, Ryan. It is what it is."

She pulled away from him and rushed up the remaining steps to the door of her building where she paused. The atmosphere between the two of them had changed in a heartbeat and he had no idea why.

When he reached her side, he looked down into her face. Her eyes, which had been gleaming with desire when he helped her out of the car, were now stormy, any hint of heat gone.

What the hell?

Before Suzie, if a girl changed emotions quicker than a flash of lightning he would shrug it off and see if he could sweet talk her into a better mood. He had an idea that any attempt to sweet talk Suzie would be squashed before he'd even started. Surprisingly, he didn't want travel that road. What he wanted with Suzie was a true relationship in every sense of the word. A relationship where each person was respected, like his parents' relationship. His dad had cautioned him many years ago that the key to a successful relationship and marriage was always being honest with each other, even when the truth could hurt the person you loved. If you lied to them you were not only being disrespectful to yourself, you were disregarding the person you cared about the most.

If they were going to have the type of relationship he wanted, then he needed to find out what set Suzie off, because something he'd said certainly had. On the front stoop of her building wasn't the best place to have this conversation, but here they were, and they were going to talk.

"What's going, Suzie?"

"Nothing."

Ryan pinched the bridge of his nose, she was pricklier than a prickle bush in the middle of a jungle. Both required him to step carefully through to get safely to the other side. "Nothing is the same as fine. There's something. Talk to me, Roses. Help me understand what I said to upset you. And I know it's something I said."

Tension slid out of her and her body swayed toward his, he caught her and wrapped his arms around her. God, it was so perfect holding her tightly against him. He brushed his lips across the top of her head. "Let's go upstairs and talk," he suggested. "That is if you still want me to come in."

A shudder rippled through her. "Yes, I still want you to come up."

"Thank you."

Together they walked into the building and headed for the elevator. The trip to her floor was made in silence, the elevator taking its sweet time. If the circumstances between them had been different he may have used the slow trip to reacquaint himself with her lips. The kiss they'd shared before walking into Robot's backyard had been playing on repeat in his mind the whole time they were there.

Now he wanted to take it further.

Hand in hand they walked down the hall to her apartment, Suzie's heart racing with every step they took. Anticipation built inside of her with regards to what was going to happen next. The door at the end opened and Jeffery stuck his head out. Immediately Ryan tensed beside her. If she hadn't been connected to him through their hands and so tuned into him, she would've missed the action. She couldn't deny having a big sexy Navy SEAL beside her gave her a sense of security when facing Jeffery.

"Hey Suzie, you okay?" The question was a simple one, however for the first time since Jeffery had taken it upon himself to speak to her all the time, there was a hint of anger in his tone. His gaze had zeroed in on their joined hands.

"Yep, Jeffery, everything's fine. Goodnight." She could see he wanted to say something more to her, but instead he slammed the door shut.

"I really don't like that guy," Ryan muttered as she slipped the key into the lock.

"I'm sure he's just being an extra diligent neighbor. I bet he does this for everyone who lives the apartments around him." Suzie wasn't sure if she was trying to convince herself or Ryan with that comment. From memory, Jeffery hadn't said boo to anyone else on this floor except her.

"Are you trying to convince me or yourself?"

Damn, how had he known that was exactly what I was thinking?

Instead of answering she unlocked her door. Before she could step through Ryan pulled on the hand that still had possession of hers. "What?"

"Let me check it out before you go in."

She rolled her eyes and tugged her hand free of his. "Seriously? If I hadn't invited you up, you wouldn't have been here to do this."

Ryan leaned in close and she shivered at his intense look, the gold flecks in his hazel eyes warming her. "I always walk my date to her door."

Suzie grabbed the door frame to stop herself from melting. The first time they'd met she never would've picked him as a guy who could be romantic. But with a simple sentence he showed her what he was capable of.

God, she wanted to kiss him. Wanted to feel his lips on hers again. He'd practically devoured her when they'd arrived at Robot's place. It had been a miracle she'd been able to form coherent sentences the first half hour of their visit. But here they were, in her apartment with her bed calling to her like a siren's call.

Giving into her needs, ones she'd denied herself since Ryan had come back into her life, she lifted her arms and looped them around his neck. She aligned her body against his. How much he wanted her evident by the hard ridge resting against her stomach.

"You really don't want to check the whole apartment out. The only place that needs checking on is the bedroom," she whispered as she laid her lips over his, nudging him so he stepped backward into her apartment. His arms tightened around her and he took over the kiss.

She moaned against his mouth and registered the slamming of her door before Ryan scooped her up in his arms. He pulled his lips away from hers and she chased his mouth, wanting to continue kissing him.

"Where's the bedroom, Roses?"

Yeah, he'd only been in her kitchen and living room when he'd been over for dinner. "Down the hall, last door on the left," she said before she zeroed in on his lips again.

His mouth was soft beneath hers. The urgency

that had been flowing through her at the front door had settled into a delicious hum.

Once again Ryan dragged his lips from hers and slowly lowered her to the ground, sliding her body down his. The friction the movement created fired her blood in a way being with Peter never had.

Ryan smoothed his hands down her arms until their fingertips were touching, her skin quivered at the contact. "Are you sure you want this, Suzie? I know I want it but if you want to take more time to building up to us sharing a bed again, then that's fine I'll leave right now."

As much as she tried to fight it, she fell a little in love with Ryan in that moment. To answer his question she took a step back from him, gathered the bottom of her top and pulled it up over her head. His breath hissed out and a rush of power washed over her at the way his eyes dilated upon seeing the lacy bra she wore. Her breast size had increased during her pregnancy and she normally wore more supportive bras, but today she'd wanted to feel sexy and had put on one of her nice bras. Her breasts almost spilled out of the cups.

He closed the gap between them and placed his hands on her hips, electricity zinged through her at the contact. The way her body was reacting to the slightest connection between them she could practically orgasm with another kiss. "Does this answer your question, Joker?"

"Definitely. And it's Ryan. Call me Ryan."

He lowered his head and took possession of her

lips again, fanning the flames within her until they burst over her and she felt warm from the inside out and only Ryan could extinguish the flames.

Her hands found the hem of his shirt and pulled it out of the waistband of his jeans. She couldn't wait to brush her naked body against his. It had been so long since they'd been intimate, but she remembered every second. Remembered every touch and sensation of flesh against flesh. Remembered the moment when the world stopped, and they orgasmed together.

Suzie didn't doubt that tonight was going to be even better, even though last time had an illicit feel about it seeing as they'd only just met. The chemistry between the two of them couldn't be denied. It was a once in a lifetime type of chemistry and she planned to hang onto it for as long as she could.

Her fingers plucked at the buttons until she was able to push the fabric off his shoulders. His skin burned beneath her fingers.

"More," she moaned as he worked her jeans off her. "I need more."

She sounded greedy and she didn't care. It certainly wasn't putting Ryan off as he quickly divested himself of his jeans and underwear so he stood in front of her gloriously naked while she still had her bra and panties on.

Ryan took her hand and led her the short distance to the bed, pulling her covers down with one hand before encouraging her to lie down. Before she lay down she went to unhook her bra, but Ryan stilled her movements. "That's my job," he murmured and placed a kiss between her breasts.

The last time they were together, urgency had dictated their actions. She couldn't deny that taking it slow upped the ante and heightened her emotions.

She lay down on the bed, the cotton sheets cool beneath her heated flesh. She shifted to the middle to allow Ryan the room he needed. He crawled onto the bed and ran his hand up the inside of her left leg, stopping tantalizing close to her throbbing core. He had an amazing tongue and she was hoping he would use it as wickedly has he had before.

Instead of fulfilling her silent wish, his hands and mouth totally bypassed her pussy. He blew a soft breath onto her tummy and gooseflesh bubbled over her skin. She expected him to follow that up with a kiss, but he sat back on his haunches and placed his hands over the slight bulge of her tummy.

She bit her lip as a wave of uncertainly washed over her. Irrational as it was, a million thoughts fired through her brain. Now confronted with the physical evidence of her pregnancy, bigger boobs and a rounded belly, did he find her unattractive? Did he find the whole idea of making love to her abhorrent?

A look down at his still hard cock jutting out from between his legs should've given her the answer she need, only it didn't. After never being enough for Peter. After him always telling her she needed to make more effort, at moments when she was most vulnerable, like lying practically naked in front of a hot guy, the old wounds she thought she'd sewn shut, split open.

"I can't believe that my son or daughter is growing inside of you," he redirected his gaze from her belly to her face. "Thank you, Suzie for this amazing gift."

Her breath whooshed out of her and tears gathered in the corners of her eyes. "It wasn't just me."

Ryan brushed a tear away that had leaked out of her eye. "I know, but it's your body that is nurturing and creating our child. I swear I won't let anything happen to either of you."

Suzie placed her hand over one of his. "We know that." She lifted her hips, signaling what she wanted. For half a heartbeat she wondered if Ryan was going to change his mind and hold her all night. But then he smiled and kissed her belly before trailing lower where she wanted him the most.

Her eyelids drifted shut as he blew over the top of her panties. His fingers looped around the lacy band and pulled them down her legs. She lifted her hips to help with the removal. He kissed her inner thigh again. Her body tightened anticipating the moment when he would finally give her the most intimate kiss she was craving. She didn't have to wait long, Ryan gripped her hips, holding her still as his lips closed over her. It was impossible to hold back the moan of delight as his tongue licked her slick folds. If she was being honest with herself, she'd been craving this moment again since she'd walked into the hospital room and had seen him. This was her child's father and he could've died without knowing he had a son or daughter.

Now wasn't the time to think over those few moments. What was happening to her right now was what she needed to do, to live in the moment? Ryan was here, in her bed and crawling into her heart.

His teeth nipped her sensitive bud and all her thoughts centered on the man between her legs and what he was doing to her. Her body warmed with every stroke of his tongue. Every bite on her clit. Her fingers clenched the bedsheets as the muscles within her tightened, waiting for that moment when all the tension was released in her climax. She was so close, she ground her hips against Ryan's mouth, increasing the friction until her back arched and she cried out her release. Her blood pulsed through her as she came down from the high Ryan's tongue had given her.

He crept up her body, his lips kissing her quivering flesh until he was lying over her, his hard cock nudging her entrance.

"You okay?" he asked, caressing the pale strip of skin beneath her ear lobe with his lips. She shuddered at the contact.

"No."

He pulled back, his eyes filling with concern. "Are you hurting?"

She lifted her hips, circling them so she teased his hard length. "Yes, right here. You need to heal the pain."

He groaned and entered her with the tip of his dick. "I was worried."

Suzie knew she shouldn't have teased him like that, but she couldn't help it. Tightening her arms around his shoulders she moved so he slipped a little further inside of her. "I'm wonderful, but I'd be even better if you start moving." He thrust in and she sighed out. "You feel so good, babe. So good."

He began to move slowly. Each stroke building the tension up in her again. Her hands roamed down his back until she found his firm ass, her nails digging into the firm flesh. His rhythm faltered for a second before smoothing out. She did it again to see if she got the same reaction.

Suzie yelped when his arms firmed around her and in a blur their positions were changed and she was on top of him, looking down at his chest, the perfection marred by a couple of scars. Her breath caught in her throat, her man was a warrior who risked his life every day. She was in awe his bravery.

The urgency to reach a second climax flowed out of her, replaced by the need to stretch this encounter out for as long as possible. Before she could move he pulled her off him a grimace crossing his face.

"What?" she asked. No way he was stopping their encounter, was he?

"I'm not wearing protection." Each word ground out between clenched teeth.

She laughed and placed a hand on her belly. "It's a bit late to be worrying about protection. We tried that, and it didn't work." She bent and kissed him on the lips. "We don't need it."

His tongue tangled with hers, vying to dominate

their lovemaking. She shifted herself so she could accept him back into her body, and bit back her disappointment when he pulled his mouth away from hers.

"I'm serious, Roses. It's not just about getting pregnant."

She sighed, and a spark of anger ignited in her. Was he suggesting he could catch something from her? Or she could catch something from him? She'd only ever slept with two guys in her life, her ex-husband Peter and the man she was currently lying on top of.

Ryan, on the other hand, was a big flirt, and a good looking Navy SEAL to boot. He probably had more bed partners than she wanted to think about.

"Why are we having this conversation now? It's definitely a mood killer." Although that was a lie, her body still hummed with sexual energy and the erection nudging her belly showed no signs of deflating.

"I need to keep you safe, Roses."

His sincerity melted away the anger in her. "You were the last person I slept with. I had a battery of tests when I first discovered I was pregnant. Everything came back clear. I haven't slept with anyone since that one night with you. Can you say the same?"

Ryan brushed a hand over her hair, his fingers tracing a line down her cheek until he threaded his fingers through her silky threads and cupped the back of her hair, encouraging her to get closer to him. She complied. "You were the last person I slept with too and I've just been in hospital. I've had blood transfusions. I know these days the chances of getting an infection from a transfusion is slim, but I need to know I'm protecting you and our baby. Until I know for sure, I'm not taking the risk."

As a nurse she should've taken into account his recent hospital stay, but in this room, in this bed, she was all woman. One who had the man she was craving lying underneath her. His concern was endearing and the fact he could keep his head when hers was in the clouds amazed her. "Top drawer."

While keeping her anchored to his body, Ryan reached over and pulled the drawer open. Suzie extricated herself from his hold and grabbed the square box out. It had been unopened for months, she'd grabbed it from the samples at the hospital as a *just in case*. A minute later she had the square foil packet open and was back straddling Ryan's body.

The break in action should've cooled her emotions, instead it only increased them. The anticipation of him filling her again had her fumbling as she rolled the latex over him. Once it was in place she rose up and sank back down his length. Her breath hissed out at the contact and she started moving. A slow, circular motion of her hips. She closed her eyes and tossed her head back, giving herself over to the connection they were building.

Every time she rose up, Ryan lifted his hips, chasing after her. She wanted to take it slow, savor being on top but it was too much. The base of her spine tingled with her impending release and her movements became jerky. Their bodies slapped together as they worked to reach the ultimate goal.

Her toes curled as she shattered through a release more powerful than anything she'd ever experienced before. With another thrust Ryan clamped her tight against him as he called out her name and his body shook out his climax.

Unable to keep upright she collapsed against his chest, his breathing as ragged as hers. She thought their first night together was amazing, it paled into comparison to what they just shared. This time her emotions were fully engaged. This man was the father of her child. It made the connection between them stronger and more special. A connection she didn't want to give up.

CHAPTER NINE

Ryan floated to the surface of consciousness. A distant buzzing reached his ears. Opening his eyes he took a moment to adjust to the unfamiliar surroundings. A smile broke out over his face when he heard the rustle of movement beside him.

Suzie.

He turned his head and there she lay, her gorgeous hair covering half her face and her shoulder. His fingers itched to smooth it away, but he didn't want to wake her. He'd kept her active most of the night and she needed her sleep.

The buzzing stopped, and he closed his eyes again, only for them to pop open when it sounded again. Immediately his body snapped to attention. That was his phone. Two calls in succession could only mean one thing, he had orders.

He tossed the covers back and slipped out of the

bed, cursing when his leg almost buckled beneath him. The muscles around his wound still hadn't healed properly, but he was going to fight through the discomfort.

Scooping up his pants as he walked out of the room he strode down the short hallway to the living room so he could have this conversation without disturbing Suzie.

He pulled out his device and glanced at the screen, a frown marring his forehead when he saw Tex's name flashing on the screen.

Why was he calling and what was so urgent that he had to call twice?

Ryan connected the call and stepped into his pants, disregarding the fact he didn't have underwear on. He didn't want to have this conversation naked.

"Tex? What's happening?"

"Joker, I've got the information you wanted on that guy, Jeffrey Elkin."

"I'm guessing it's bad if you're giving me back to back calls this early in the morning."

"I've called you once, the other was your Commander. I'll make this quick."

Ryan knew better than to question how Tex knew who'd called him. There was a reason so many SEAL teams worked with Tex. The guy was a computer whiz and knew things even before most of them did. He'd helped Italy in locating Erin and Antonia when they went missing. It was why he'd called the other man when he'd wanted information on Suzie's creepy neighbor. "Okay, lay it on me."

"The guy's clean. He's got three traffic violations for speeding, but they're spread out over fifteen years. He works at the local library as the head librarian."

"The guy's a librarian? Never would've guessed that. Still there's something about him Tex that doesn't feel right. He always opens his door when Suzie comes home or leaves. He did it last night when I brought her home."

"What's your gut telling you?" Tex asked and Ryan appreciated that he didn't make light of his concerns.

"That I need to watch him."

"Then do it. Always trust your gut, Joker. I'll make sure I keep a track of Suzie and I'll keep an eye on this dude, too."

"Thanks, 'ppreciate man."

"Always, brother, now I suggest you call your Commander back. And trust me, I'll do everything I can to keep your woman safe."

"Later."

Ryan disconnected the call and a second later it started buzzing in his hand. Shit, it was his Commander. He was about to raked over the coals for not calling him straight back.

Unconsciously, Ryan straightened his spine, like he would when he walked into Commander Black's office and hit the accept button. "Yes, Sir."

"Smith, get your ass to base. You're wheels up in ninety minutes. You'll get your instructions when you arrive."

"Yes, Sir."

The double beep indicated the call had ended. Ryan ran a hand through his head. He didn't have time to mess around. He needed to get home, dressed in his gear and out the door.

He rushed back to Suzie's room, stopping when his gaze fell on the smooth expanse of her back. God, how he wanted to climb back into that bed, kiss his way down his spine to wake her up. Then make slow love to her. Hear her soft cries of pleasure as he brought her to the brink and the yell of her completion as she fell into her orgasm.

His dick hardened against the metal zipper of his jeans, obviously liking the idea too, but it was one he couldn't fulfill. Ryan glanced around the room and spied a notepad and pen on her bedside table. Leaving a note wasn't the ideal thing to do, but he really didn't want to disturb her sleep.

In seconds he'd ripped the page off the pad and rested it on the pillow he'd used. He leaned down and inhaled, her sweet rose scent intermingled with the aroma of their lovemaking. He closed his eyes and savored it, before kissing her lightly on the cheek.

"I'll be back, Roses. I..." he couldn't finish the sentence. It didn't make sense to say the words out loud even though it was what he was feeling. It was too soon to say he loved her. How did he even know if he did and it wasn't just because of the great sex they'd shared? Or the baby?

Now wasn't the time to debate his feelings for Suzie. The team was about to go wheels up, his focus needed to be on the upcoming mission, his first since he'd gotten shot. He couldn't be a liability to them.

Forty minutes later Ryan marched down the hallway to the meeting room where the team usually met. He walked in and stopped. They were all standing around Italy, the last time that happened, Erin had been taken captive. Then, instead of going on their allocated mission, they'd teamed up with Wolf's team and had gone to rescue Erin and Antonia.

God, he hoped it was nothing like that. With Suzie in his life now, he couldn't imagine the pain Italy had to have in that moment. If anything happened to Suzie, he was sure he'd go insane.

"What's happened?" he asked and five men turned in his direction.

"About time you showed," responded Cowboy.

He grunted and made his way to stand near Italy. They guy had a dumbfounded, shocked look on his face. "Is Erin okay, man?"

A big smile broke out over his face. "More than okay. I'm gonna be a dad."

Ryan bit his tongue to stop himself from blurting out *Me too.* Instead he slapped him on the back. "Congrats, man, that's awesome. Does this mean our orders are changed, we're not leaving now?" He hoped that was the case, then he could stay and keep a close eye on Suzie.

"Nah, she told me to get out of her hair when I suggested I stay around. She said she was fine and if something was going to happen it wouldn't matter if I was nearby or in the middle of nowhere."

Italy's tone suggested that it would kill him if something happened while he was away. Ryan knew exactly how the other man felt. "I'm sure everything's going be fine. After the hell you two went through to be together. Nothing's going to happen Erin or your kid."

Italy nodded, and conversation died when Commander Black strode through the door.

"Gentleman, we've got a situation in the Congo. You'll be joining with another team. You'll see them on the plane."

Commander Black continued to give a rundown of the mission. Ryan listened with half an ear, his mind on what Suzie would think when she woke up alone. Would she hate him for not waking her or would she understand he was thinking of her?

An elbow to his ribs pulled him from his thoughts, he glared at Robot who simply raised his eyebrows. Yeah, he didn't need to get on the bad side of his team his first mission back. With a concerted effort he redirected thoughts of Suzie out of his mind and on the task at hand. He didn't want to be the reason the mission failed.

When the Commander finished relaying information about the trip, Ryan and his team walked out and headed toward the airfield.

"Are you going to be okay?" Robot asked as he walked beside him.

Ryan bristled at the suggestion that he would be a liability. "Yeah I'm fine. I can deal with anything."

Robot studied him, and Ryan schooled his features into an impassive face. It must have worked because his team lead gave a brief nod and they continued on their way.

"Do you think it's Wolf's team we'll be working with?" he asked.

Robot shrugged. "Who knows, could be anyone."

They reached the plane and climbed onboard. Already seated were eight men dressed in black. Ryan recognized one of the guys as the one who sat next to him on the flight back after he got shot. He wasn't too hard to forget with the scar marring one side of his face. He sat next to him and held out his hand. "Truck, right? Good to see you?"

The man nodded and grasped Ryan's hand, giving it a quick shake. "Yeah, good to see you on your feet."

"Thanks." Ryan settled his pack next on the ground next to him. He glanced around at the other guys. Last time he'd been dealing with pain so hadn't paid too much attention to the other team. Now, getting a good look at them, he could tell they weren't another SEAL team. These guys carried a harder edge about them. They were probably Delta Force, but he knew better than to ask.

From the brief they'd been given by the Commander, Ryan had guessed it was going to be a tough mission. With a Delta Force team along, things just got a bit more interesting.

Susie woke up and stretched, her muscles protesting at the movement. She reached out and found an empty side, the sheets cool between her touch.

She lay still, hoping to hear the sound of the shower, or movement in the kitchen. But silence shrouded her. She was alone.

Why would Ryan leave without saying goodbye to her? Did their night together mean absolutely nothing to him?

Stop it!

He wouldn't leave without a good reason. She flung her hand out to grab the pillow he used to hug close to her when she heard the crinkle of paper. Sitting up she clutched the sheet against her breast and picked up the note.

Hey Roses,

Sorry to run out without waking you, but I got orders. I don't know how long I'll be and if I can even call you. If you need anyone or anything call Erin.

I'll call the moment I can.

Ryan xxx

Suzie read the note a couple of times. Okay, so he

didn't run out on her, but she wished he'd woken her up. Even to say goodbye. What if she never heard his voice again?

She slammed the brakes on thoughts like that. No way was she going to let her fears paralyze her. This was the way her life was going to be if she wanted Ryan in her future. A glance at the clock told her she needed to get a move on if she was going to make her shift at the hospital.

"We've got this, baby," she said as she patted her stomach. "No matter what, Mommy is going to be strong for you and for Ryan." There was no other choice, falling apart every time Ryan left wouldn't be good for her or their child. They were all a team and, as he said, she could contact Erin. The other woman must be feeling very vulnerable knowing she'd just found out she was pregnant, and her man was leaving her behind for goodness knows how long.

Determined to be the strong, independent woman she'd become after walking away from Peter, she threw back the covers and got out of bed. Her stomach turned over and for a moment she thought she was going to throw up. She was in her second trimester, she should be over this. Although it wasn't unheard of that women suffered morning sickness throughout the whole of their pregnancy. A couple of deep breaths pushed the nausea away. She had this.

Thirty minutes later she was munching on an apple checking she had everything in her handbag, she'd put Ryan's note in a safe place. It comforted her to keep it close to her.

Opening the door, she gasped and choked on the piece of apple she'd been chewing. A large slap on the back dislodged the piece. Tears streamed down her face and she gulped air down like a goldfish out of water. "Jesus, Jeffrey, what the hell do you think you're doing standing at my front door?"

"I was about to knock to see if you were okay. You've normally left work by now when you have your morning shift."

Apprehension prickled down her spine and Ryan's words about not trusting him resonated in her mind. "How do you know what shift I'm on?"

"If you were on night shift you wouldn't have been out last night."

His quick response was reasonable, and made sense, however his actions were beginning to creep her out. He bobbed his head around as if he was trying to see inside her apartment. He wouldn't find anyone. He had no idea Ryan had slipped out earlier, or did he?

"Can I help you with anything else?" she asked, wanting to put some distance between them. Until Ryan had talked about Jeffrey last night she hadn't given the other man too much head space.

"No, just making sure you're okay."

"Well, as you can see I'm fine. I need to go, otherwise I'll be late." She closed the door and twisted the lock, wishing Jeffrey had walked away. She hated knowing he was aware her apartment was empty. Of course, this wasn't the first time they'd met up in the hall when she'd left for work. Only this time it wasn't a coincidence. Everything about this encounter screamed he'd been watching her.

A shudder rippled down her spine and she wished Ryan wasn't away. No way was she planning on letting Jeffrey know he wasn't going to be around for a while. There was no way she could shake him off. He was going to trail her to the lifts and out the building—like he'd done on numerous occasions.

The trip down to the ground floor, passed in silence. That was the last thing she expected to happen. What she expected was for Jeffrey to pepper her with questions about Ryan and where he was. It seemed totally weird that he hadn't especially after he'd asked her if she was alone.

"Have a good day at work, Jeffrey." Suzie made to walk away, but a hand on her arm stilled her. Unlike when Ryan touched her, her skin shriveled instead of sizzling. As impolite as it would seem, she shook her arm free and took a couple of steps back. "You wanted something?"

He swallowed, and his eyes shifted left to right. "I, uh, wanted to know if you'd like to have a drink with me tonight."

He was asking her on a date? After he'd seen Ryan arrive home with her last night. The guy was delusional if he thought she would go out with him. Instinct had her wanting to yell *No* loudly at him. She controlled the urge, upsetting the man wouldn't achieve anything. She had to let him down lightly.

"Thank you for the invitation, but I'm going to have to decline. I already have plans with a girlfriend." She didn't have plans, but she was going to ring Erin and see if she could spend the night with her. Even though she'd only met the girl, the fact that their men were away, she was sure Erin would be okay with her crashing at her place. She had an afternoon shift tomorrow, so she could slip home when Jeffrey was safely at work.

His eyes narrowed as if he didn't trust her words. "Okay, maybe another night then."

"Maybe." She glanced at her watch. "I really have to run, thanks for making sure I made it downstairs safely."

"Anytime, Suzie, I only ever want to keep you safe."

Somehow, she figured her sense of safe was different to his. Brushing off the encounter she walked to her car, darting a glance over her shoulder, noticing that he stood on the pavement watching her.

"Damn it, Ryan. Why did you have to go and leave now?" she muttered as she got into her car.

Today was going to be long day.

CHAPTER TEN

Erin flopped down on the couch and Suzie bit back a laugh. "I'm gonna kill, Carlos when he gets back."

Now Suzie laughed. "No, you're not. Can I get you anything?"

"A time machine so I can leap forward four months. I thought they called it *morning sickness* for a reason, you know you get sick when you wake up, not at fucking 9 p.m. in the evening."

When Suzie had called the other woman, Erin had been more than happy to have her over for the night.

"Here, I made you some ginger tea." Antonia walked in with a steaming mug in her hand.

"Ginger is good for nausea," Susie agreed.

"I'd prefer a wine," grumbled Erin as she accepted the mug from her friend.

"Well, you had to go and get yourself knocked up, don't blame me for your lack of ability to have wine."

Erin poked her tongue out at her friend and a dart of jealousy pierced Suzie. She wished she had a girlfriend who would look out for her like Antonia was for Erin. When she'd arrived at Erin's place she'd been surprised to see Antonia was there. As far as Suzie was aware, Antonia had a job in New York.

"Once you've had the baby we can go out and have a celebratory drink," Suzie said.

"You'll at least you'll get to have wine sooner than me."

"You're pregnant, too?" asked Antonia her eyes wide in surprise.

It was impossible to prevent the blush warming her cheeks. Words were impossible, so she just nodded.

Now two people who were associated with Ryan knew she was pregnant. Had he told anyone on his team? Erin had mentioned that Carlos had gone off to base with a goofy grin on his face, so him keeping it quiet was going to be impossible. Would Ryan then also spread the news?

No, he wouldn't. She may have only known Ryan for a short time, but there was no way he'd take away the limelight from Carlos. He'd let the other man enjoy his moment before he'd break the news. Besides the last thing the team needed to know before heading out on an assignment was that two of the team members had expectant significant others.

"Suzie? I asked if Joker is the father?" Antonia interrupted her thoughts.

"Umm yeah, he is."

"But didn't you just meet?"

"Leave it, Antonia." Erin interjected.

Antonia's questioning didn't bother her. Suzie was well aware Ryan had wanted to meet Antonia after seeing her picture. He'd told her about it their first dinner date. It had surprised her how honest he'd been, and she appreciated it. Besides he'd also mentioned that Antonia had spent most of her visit with Robot and not him. There had been no spark between him and Antonia, even though Ryan had like her in the picture, in person they just weren't compatible. Not like her and Ryan.

A shiver rippled through her in remembrance of their first date and the night they'd just shared together.

"It's okay, Erin. I don't mind the questions." Suzie looked over at Antonia who'd settled in the lounge chair, her legs curled up beneath her. "I met Ryan when you and Erin were brought into the hospital after your kidnapping. We had dinner and well one thing lead to another and here we are about to be parents."

"You have no reason to be annoyed, Toni, you told me you didn't feel anything with Joker *and* you said he agreed."

If she hadn't been watching Antonia closely she wouldn't have seen the momentary flash of hurt appear in her eyes. Shit, did she feel something for

Ryan? Was that what she and Robot were arguing about yesterday at the party? Or was she hurt that Erin called her out.

The last thing Suzie wanted to do was cause issues between two friends. Before she could say anything, Erin spoke again.

"Plus, there's something going on with you and Robot, and you still haven't told me what that's all about."

"It's complicated," Antonia responded.

"Isn't it always," said Suzie. "Whoever tells you their relationships are perfect are lying. Believe me I know."

She clamped her lips shut. The last thing she wanted to do was talk about her disaster of a marriage and how she'd let a man control every single aspect of her life. Suzie still wasn't convinced once the baby came, Ryan would try and control everything. No matter how much he told her she was in charge.

"Preaching to the choir, sister," Erin said as she leaned forward holding her hand up for a high five. Their palms slapped and the tension that had enveloped the room disappeared. Suzie also noticed Antonia breathed out. The issue between her and Robot was definitely interesting, but it wasn't her place to question her about it. She redirected the conversation onto the latest hot new cop show on television and received a grateful mouthed *thank you* from Antonia.

The second she closed her apartment door, Suzie slumped against the wood, her heart-rate falling back to normal. The whole time she walked down the hallway she kept waiting for Jeffrey's door to open, which was ridiculous since it was the middle of the morning and he would've been at work.

A yawn wracked her body. The evening with Erin and Antonia had been fun and there were no more awkward moments. They'd shared their celebrity crushes and at about two in the morning they decided it was time to sleep. Only sleep had proven difficult for Suzie. Her mind immediately drifted to Ryan and she wondered where he was and what he was doing. Was he safe? Had he been hurt again?

It had taken a monumental effort to push the thoughts aside and finally fall asleep. Being exhausted wasn't good for her or the baby, especially since she had a shift she had to get through.

Dragging herself away from the doorway she looked up, stopped and gasped—her apartment had been trashed. The stuffing from her couch throw pillows were scattered all over the hallway.

With trembling fingers she reached into her purse, pulled out her cell phone and dialed 9-1-1. She stayed rooted to the spot while she gave her address and other details to the dispatcher.

What she wanted to do was get out of there, but she had to now wait. The thing was her door wasn't ajar when she arrived home. The lock didn't appear to have been tampered with.

On shaky legs she walked down the hallway, ignoring the urge to pick up the pillows.

All the contents of her fridge and cupboards had been tossed to the ground in her kitchen. Plates shattered. How had nobody heard that racket and called the police? The walls in her apartment weren't soundproof. The last place she wanted to walk into was her bedroom, but she had to. If this is what they'd done to her kitchen what the hell had they done to her bedroom.

The door to her room stood wide open and she stopped on the threshold, biting the inside of her cheek hard, tasting blood when she saw the word SLUT painted on her wall.

God, she wished Ryan was here. She wanted to wrap herself in his arms and ask him to take her away from this.

Who had invaded her privacy like this? Why had they done it?

She let out a yelp when her phone rang, she looked at the screen but didn't recognize the number. She was going to ignore it but wondered if it could be the police calling her.

"Hello?" Her voice shook on the simple word and she hated herself for sounding so pathetic.

"Is this Suzie Waterson?" The owner of the voice had a smooth, reassuring tone.

"Yes. Who is this?" There, now that sounded better.

"My name is Tex Keegan. I'm a friend of Joker's you placed a 9-1-1 call. Is everything okay?"

Now that was creepy, and on top of the break-in, it was almost too much for her to handle.

"How do you know that? And how do I know you even know Joker?" No way was she going to say Ryan's name, in case she was actually talking to the guy who committed the break-in.

His chuckle rolled down the line. Not a way to inject confidence in her. "I'd have been annoyed if you hadn't questioned me and accepted me on my word. Why don't you text, Erin, she can vouch for me? I'll wait while you do it."

The man was a contradiction, all arrogant and sure of himself, but his voice was soothing and calming. She would send a text to Erin. "Who did you say you were?"

"Tex Keegan, former United States Navy SEAL."

Suzie pulled the phone away from her ear and opened her texting app, quickly typing out a message.

ERIN, DO YOU KNOW A TEX KEEGAN?

She hit send and hoped Erin didn't have her head over the toilet bowl and would answer her message quickly. No sooner had she finished the thought her phone beeped in her hand.

YEP, SURE DO. WHY?

HE CALLED ME BECAUSE HE SAW I CALLED 9-1-1.

WHAT???? YOU CALLED 9-1-1 WHY?

She chuckled at Erin's all caps message. How could she laugh when her home had been invaded? Maybe she was going into shock.

Suzie could see the little three dots indicating Erin

was firing off another message so she quickly typed one of her own.

I came home and found my place trashed. I'm waiting for the police to turn up.

I'm coming over. I'll be there as soon as I can. And trust Tex. He's one of the good guys. Like our guys.

Her fingers hovered over the keypad to tell her not to come over, but she couldn't deny it would be good to see a friendly face.

Closing her eyes and rolling her shoulders to alleviate the tension building in them, Suzie brought the phone to your ear. "Erin says I can trust you."

Once again the man laughed. "Good. Tell me everything? I know Joker's away and he'd have my ass if he knew I didn't try and help you."

"Once a SEAL always a SEAL? That's what he told me once."

"Yes, I do everything I can to keep an eye on my brothers and their women."

The proprietorship of his words should've bothered her, considering everything she'd gone through with Peter, but they didn't. They had the opposite effect, they gave her the strength to face the disaster that was her apartment.

"Thank you, Tex. I appreciate it."

"Welcome. You still haven't told me what happened."

Suzie sighed. "I came home from spending the night with Erin and found my place trashed. It's a disaster and my bed…"

"What? You can tell me anything," he said gently.

"Whoever they were painted the word Slut on my bedroom wall."

Tex let out a string of curses that would've shocked if she hadn't heard them all before from the patient's she dealt with at the hospital.

"Shit," she blurted out.

"What?"

"I'm supposed to work in a couple of hours."

"I suggest you call them. Do it now and I'll call you back in five minutes and we can talk about who could've done this to you."

"Okay, and Tex?"

"Yes?"

"Thank you." Her eyes filled with tears at how a complete stranger had made her feel like she wasn't alone in the world.

"It's what I do. We'll find out who did this, Suzie."

She nodded, even though Tex couldn't see her. If she spoke she was afraid she'd break down in a torrent of tears and she couldn't do that. Not yet.

Ryan traipsed through the Congo, slapping at the bugs that flew into his face. "Fucking hell," he muttered.

A chuckle sounded behind him, he glanced over at the painted face of Truck, the Delta Force guy he'd been paired with. "Annoying fuckers, aren't they?"

"Tell me about it." He scratched the back of his neck again, this time it wasn't from a bug bite.

"What's up, Joker? That's about the tenth time in the last fifteen minutes you've scratched your neck."

Ryan stopped. Truck did as well. He looked at the other man, knowing he'd understand what he said next. "I don't know, I've got a feeling something's up."

Immediately Truck tensed. "With the mission?"

"I don't think so."

"You got a woman back home?" asked Truck, his eyes scanning the area they stood in.

"Yeah."

"She by herself or with friends?"

Ryan went to rub his hand down his face, but stopped, it was covered in black paint for a reason. "I'm not sure. I left her a note and told her to call Erin."

"A note, dude? That's harsh."

Ryan started walking again, they were on a mission not a fucking picnic break. Truck walked alongside him. "She was asleep. I didn't want to wake her." He blew out a breath and braced himself to impart news he hadn't even told his team. "She's pregnant. She needed her sleep."

"Shit, remind me not to hang around here too long. There's something in the water. First Italy and now you. Congratulations." The big man held out a closed fist, Ryan fist bumped it.

"Thanks. I haven't known long. So that's why I haven't said anything to the team."

"Got it. Your woman got any issues that may have you on edge?"

"Suzie. Her name's Suzie and yeah she's got a neighbor that I don't have a good feeling about."

Truck opened his mouth to speak but then slammed it shut and crouched down indicating Ryan should do the same. They both ducked below the overhang from the trees and Ryan focused on what was around him. He slowed his breathing until he was hardly making a sound.

There, in the distance the distinct crunch of a twig snapping. Then another. Whoever was coming wasn't hiding their approach. Ryan checked his rifle and clicked the safety off. Through silent communication Truck took up an opposite position to him. Both sets of eyes tracking the area.

The footsteps got louder. Ryan's heart-rate kicked up a notch, adrenaline spiking through him. The person was almost upon them when they stopped. His finger bent and flexed against the trigger, waiting for the moment when he would have to depress the piece of metal in order to save himself and Truck.

A quick look to his left and Truck was no longer there. What the fuck? Why had he left him? That wasn't how things were done on missions, you always had someone's back.

Fuck.

He couldn't let it bother him, if he allowed it to it could mean the difference between life and death. No way was he fucking dying in a jungle, not with Suzie and their baby waiting at home.

The footsteps started up again, he could see the person approaching. He lay flat on his belly, gun trained on the spot between a couple of bushes, he would have a split second to find out if they were friend or foe.

A hail of bullets rained the air before the body of the insurgent tumbled down the small rise. Truck appeared in the small gap and gave him a thumbs up.

The tension that had been spiraling tighter and tighter released like the air escaping from a balloon. He should've known Truck wouldn't have left him behind. He'd done the man a disservice by even allowing the through to cross his mind.

All he knew was, he couldn't wait to get out of this hellhole.

Two hours later he and Truck turned up at the meeting point first. Ryan slung his pack off and rolled his shoulders.

"Here," Truck called, and Ryan looked up in time to see a black object being tossed his way. He juggled it but managed not to drop it.

"What is it?"

"Secure satellite phone, call Tex. Press speed dial one." The other man turned and walked away giving Ryan his privacy.

How Truck knew Tex would have any information on Suzie shouldn't have surprised him. Once you asked Tex for help, he always watched your back. Besides the ex-SEAL had told Ryan he would watch Suzie for him.

He drummed his fingers on his thigh as he waited for the call to connect. "Truck, what's wrong?"

"It's not Truck, it's Joker."

"Ahh, she's fine…Now."

Dread pooled in his stomach. "What do you mean now? What happened? Is the baby okay?"

"Yes, to both. She's staying at Erin's."

"Well, fuck, what's with the *now* comment."

"Her place was trashed. From what she told me nothing was left untouched. The police came and took a report and dusted for prints. Erin came and took her back to her place. Don't worry I've got eyes on them. I'm making sure they're safe."

"God dammit. Fuck. I knew something was wrong." He began pacing in small circles, wishing he was anywhere but stuck in the fucking jungle.

"Joker. Keep your focus on the mission. Trust me when I say I've got this end covered."

Tex was right. He couldn't let this get to him, even though it was eating away at him that he hadn't been there to protect her or provide the support she needed. He closed his eyes and breathed in and out, getting his head back into the head space it needed to be to keep himself safe so that he could get home to Suzie and their baby.

"Thanks, man. I owe you."

"You don't owe many anything. You're my brother I take care of you and your families."

Ryan disconnected the call and tapped the phone on his leg.

"Everything okay?" asked Truck.

"Suzie's place was broken into, he says she's staying with Erin. But she and the baby are fine. That's all that matters."

"Baby?" Italy rushed up to him, anxiety written all over his face. "Is Erin okay? And where the fuck did you get a phone?"

"Erin's fine. Suzie's place was trashed. I just spoke to Tex and he said everything's fine and the phone belongs to Truck."

"But you said, baby. Who's baby?"

It looked like now was the time to share the news. "Yeah, I did, and the baby's mine. Suzie's pregnant too."

CHAPTER ELEVEN

Warm arms enclosed her, and Suzie snuggled into the embrace. A familiar spicy scent assailed her senses and her eyes popped open. This wasn't a dream. There was a hard, familiar body behind her.

"Ryan?" she mumbled.

"Yeah, Roses, I'm back. Go back to sleep. I'll be here when you wake."

"Promise?"

"I promise." His lips caressed the back of her neck and his hand rubbed her swelling stomach. Contentment washed over her, and she fell back asleep.

A few hours later she swam toward the surface of consciousness, still wrapped up in Ryan's arms. She stretched and wiggled back, her ass connecting with his morning erection.

"You are so beautiful when you wake up," he murmured as he tightened his hold on her.

"Morning breath and bed hair, yeah real attractive."

"When you wake up in dirt for the third straight day with the same six men, bed hair and morning breath is nothing."

Suzie shifted so that she was facing him. Her eyes devouring the face that had been front and center of her dreams for the last three weeks. "I missed you."

That hadn't been what she was going to say, but now the words were out she didn't regret saying them at all.

"I missed you too." His hands cupped her belly again. "How's junior doing?"

"Junior is getting bigger and he is fine."

"He? We're having a boy?"

She shook her head. "I still don't know. My doctor's appointment is today."

"I haven't missed any? What time today?"

The excitement in Ryan's voice was infectious. "No, you haven't missed any and if you can make it, my appointment is at three."

"I'll be there. I was worried after I spoke to Tex and he told me about the break-in."

Suzie sat up in bed, pulling the sheet tight around her. "You spoke to Tex? When? He didn't tell me he'd spoken to you. I didn't even know he could get in touch with you."

"I spoke to him the day it happened. I had a feeling something was off and the guy I was with had a sat phone. Believe me when I say it's very unusual for there to be any contact while on a mission. Any sort of transmission could be intercepted and put us in danger."

"Then why the hell did you call?" She punched him on the arm, irritated that he put his life in danger.

"Hey, I was worried. It was only the one call. Tex told me you were safe here with Erin and he was keeping an eye on you."

Keeping an eye on her was an understatement the man had phoned her every day. Checking in he called it. More like checking up on her. But she couldn't deny she liked it. If she couldn't have Ryan by her side knowing another big SEAL had her 'six' as he called it had made her feel better. Erin said that once you were on Tex's radar, you were on there for life so she should just get used to it.

Another realization struck her. She was still at Erin's and Ryan was in bed bedside her. "Is that how you knew I was still here? You called Tex?"

"Yeah we were wheels down around six last night and before the team went into our debriefing meeting, I called Tex and he told me where you were." He gathered her close. "I'm sorry about your place, Roses. I'm sorry I wasn't here to be the support you needed."

Tears welled in her eyes and spilled over. She burrowed her face into Ryan's solid chest, seeking comfort only he could give her.

God, she had acting like a weak woman. She thought she was done weeping like a baby when she thought about her place. She hadn't been back since the morning she'd walked in and found it trashed. She hadn't been about to face the devastation nor the feeling of never being safe again. Erin had been more than happy for her to stay at her and Carlos's place. She'd been able to help Erin when her morning sickness was severe. But now Ryan was back, and she supposed she needed to go back to her place. A shudder ripped through her at the thought.

"What's wrong?"

"I was just thinking, now you guys are back I will probably have to go back to my place. Erin has Carlos now and Antonia will be staying here in a week when she moves down from New York."

"Antonia's moving here?"

That was what he heard—that Antonia was moving here? She knew Antonia had no claim on Ryan, but even though he'd told her that first night that there was nothing between him and Antonia, did he want there to be?

"Yes, she is. Why does this interest you so much? Do you want to be with her?" She'd gone from weepy woman to jealous bitch in ten seconds.

"The only person I want to be with is the woman in my arms." He hooked a finger under her chin and lifted it until she was looking into his eyes. "I want you, Roses. No one else."

He didn't give her an opportunity to answer him as his lips descended on hers. Her arms wound around his neck and she sighed in pleasure. With their lips connected, his arms slid down her body and slipped under the satin chemise she'd worn to bed a tried and true cliché floated through the fog of lust enveloping her *absence makes the heart grow fonder*. And for her it had. As much as she'd tried to fight it, she couldn't deny it any longer. She beginning to fall for Ryan. The father of her baby. Her Navy SEAL and instead of frightening her, it empowered her.

Suzie clutched Ryan's hand tightly as they walked down the hallway to her apartment. The door at the end of the hallway opened and Jeffrey rushed out.

"Suzie, are you okay? I heard about the break-in. I wished I'd been here to help you."

Her big Navy SEAL stiffened beside her and she was transported back to the other time she'd come home with Ryan and Jeffrey had greeted them. Tex had asked her if she thought Jeffrey could be responsible for the break-in, but she'd denied it. True, he'd been acting creepy but she didn't think Jeffrey was violent. She'd seen violence once with her ex-husband. Jeffrey was a little weird. She'd come to that conclusion while Ryan was away. The man was harmless and probably had a crush on her. Or was she just kidding herself? Still she wasn't going to antagonize the man.

"Thanks Jeffrey, but it's probably safer you weren't anywhere near the place when this happened. Whoever it was could've hurt you and I would've felt guilty." Ryan's fingers tightened on her waist. Jeffrey hadn't even looked at the tall man by her side.

Ryan cleared his throat and stepped in front of her, as though he was guarding her from Jeffrey. "Thanks for your concern, but Suzie's got me now. I take care of my own."

Suzie bristled at the possessive tone in Ryan's voice. She maybe having his child and may have stayed with his teammate's fiancé, but she was still her own woman.

Clearly the other man recognized the claim Ryan was staking as Jeffrey's shoulders straightened and his chest puffed out a little. In comparison to Ryan, he was a little robin standing up to an eagle. "Suzie is my friend. I have a right to be concerned about her."

The last thing she wanted was for Ryan and Jeffrey to go at it in the middle of the hallway. The situation needed to be defused and defused now. "I appreciate it, Jeffrey. Ryan is just being a little…" *Overpowering, arrogant, sexy and protective.* None of those adjectives would work. "Well, he's worried that's all. Have a good day, Jeffrey."

She hoped he would take the hint and go back to his apartment or go off to work. After a heated second he turned on his heel and marched back to his apartment. The door slamming when it closed.

Her shoulders slumped and the tension riding her spine dissipated when Ryan rubbed his hand across her shoulders. "I'm sorry," he said as he leaned down and kissed the back of her neck. "I don't trust him, and I get all—"

"Macho Navy SEAL. I can look after myself you know." Well she thought she could until her privacy was invaded and destroyed. Now she still couldn't twist the knob to open the door.

"You know you don't have to do this," said Ryan as though he could read her mind. "The guys and I can come and clean up for you."

That was the last thing she wanted, his team traipsing down the hallway scaring not only Jeffrey but the other residents with their military bigness. This was her place and she would face it. Then put it all behind her and try and find a new place to live. No way was she going to bring a child back to a complex where break-ins could go unnoticed. "No, I need to do this." She turned so she was facing Ryan, his presence crowded her. "I told myself when I walked away from my marriage that I wouldn't be a victim anymore. I'm not going to start now."

Ryan's eyes widened at her declaration. "You've been married before? Are you saying your ex-husband *hurt* you? Why am I just finding out about this now?"

Again, not a conversation she wanted to have out where all and sundry could hear it. With a burst of courage, she twisted the knob behind her and pushed the door open.

"Fuck."

Suzie wasn't surprised by Ryan's outburst, with her back to the apartment she could still picture the devastation. "Yeah."

"You are never coming back here again," he declared as he grabbed her hand and together they walked across the threshold.

"I'd already worked that out."

"We'll go apartment hunting or house hunting next weekend. I'm sure we'll find something that we both like."

Both like?

"Whoa, wait up. Who said anything about moving in together?" While she was glad it appeared Ryan had forgotten his surprise and questions about her marriage, his assumption that they would be moving in together set her off. She extracted her hand from his and put some space between them.

"It makes sense. We're having a baby together. Why wouldn't we live together?"

Confusion colored his face, but all Suzie was focused on was his declaration about them moving in together. "Umm because you've made this decision without asking me. Did you forget you said I was in charge of how things went between the two of us. I'm not being forced into a situation where I lose all control. If that's what you think is going to happen then there's the door buddy, you can see yourself out."

Suzie stomped down the hallway to her bedroom in the hopes that she could salvage some clothes. She'd stay in a hotel if she had to. It was her life and she was still in control of it.

Ryan ran a hand over his head and counted to ten. Her anger made no sense? Why couldn't she understand he needed to keep her close, so he could protect her and their baby? He could blame it on the shock of seeing the state of her apartment on top of her declaration that she'd been married before and, if he read between the lines correctly, she'd been abused. His protective instincts had gone on high alert and he'd acted like a caveman by making decisions without even consulting her. No wonder she stormed away.

He had to fix this. Life without Suzie in it wasn't one he wanted to contemplate living.

Making his way over tossed furniture and cushions he headed for her bedroom, stopping abruptly when he spied the word painted on her wall. The woman he cared for more and more each day stood staring at the word, a tattered t-shirt in her hand. "Suzie," he called her name quietly, not wanting to scare her.

"I'm not a slut," she whispered. "I've only ever slept with two men in my life."

Ryan rushed over to her and enveloped her in a big hug, hoping to transfer some of his warmth and strength into her. "Baby, I know." He brushed a kiss on the top of her head. He didn't want to ask the question, but he had to. "Do you think it was your ex who did this? Do you think he found out about us and our baby?"

Suzie shuddered in his arms. "I don't know. I don't think so. But Peter was very good at using his words to make deep cuts into my self-confidence, so he could be responsible."

"Did you give his name to the police when they came and took their report?"

She shook her head. "I wasn't really thinking clearly and, honestly, it never crossed my mind until you asked." Suzie pulled away from his embrace and tossed the t-shirt onto the wrecked bed. "How stupid is that? He should've been my first suspect in all of this. But," she looked around. "This was done by someone in a massive rage, and that's not really Peter. His methods tended to be more on the sly. Saying things which, on the surface, didn't appear to be hurtful, but over time the cutting remarks dug deeper and deeper until nothing was left, and you ended up believing you were more worthless than a spec of dirt."

Ryan clenched his fists to stop himself from punching the wall. How could anyone do that to a person? Especially a woman who was as beautiful and full of life as Suzie. As much as he'd like to hunt the fucker down, it wouldn't achieve anything. Suzie had found the courage to walk away and he'd found her.

She was his now and he would do everything to keep her safe.

"Perhaps we should go down to the station and give them Peter's name," he suggested.

"I suppose. But I really don't think it's him. The one and only time he hit me, I walked out. The verbal abuse was something I took. It was stupid that I put up with it for so long. It was only when he decided to strike out at me, I found the strength to leave." She turned in a small circle. "This was the first place I'd truly created as my own and now it's all gone. This was my salvation and my healing process. With every piece of furniture. Every dish. Every cushion and sheet set I picked out I was putting myself back together and becoming an independent woman. Now it's all gone. In one fell swoop everything I'd built shattered beyond repair." Her voice choked up and his heart broke at seeing the tears silently tracking down her cheeks. "What did I do to deserve this?"

The sobs broke then, and he pulled her close, wrapping her up in his embrace again. He rested his cheek on top of her head, not saying anything. Just holding her and letting her cry. Reining in his desire to find this Peter guy and belt the shit out of him. No man should ever touch a woman in anger.

If he ever found who did this to her place, he wouldn't be responsible for the hurt he'd inflict on them.

He would be here for Suzie in any way shape or form to take the burden she was willing to share with him. After what she'd told him, about how her ex had treated her, he wouldn't pressure her to move in with him. He would stand by his words of her being in charge of their relationship. Every move they made would be according to Suzie. However long she needed to feel comfortable enough to live with him, he would give it to her. Be it six months or two years. She'd have it.

Suzie was his now. He planned on giving her the world.

CHAPTER TWELVE

Once again Suzie found herself lying on her back with a scratchy hospital blanket covering her legs. Ryan had hold of her hand.

"You okay, Roses?"

He'd been so wonderful after she melted down at her place. He'd held her and let her cry. Her emotions were still close to the surface, but the excitement at the prospect of seeing her baby again was taking top billing. "Yeah, I'm fine. Nervous."

Ryan scooted his chair closer to the bed. He was being so sweet she didn't know how to handle it. "What are you nervous about?" he asked.

Could she share her worries with him? Of course, she could. He was the father of her child. They were embarking on a relationship. If they didn't end up together it was important that they got on for the sake of their child. She took a deep breath and squeezed his hand. "There are so many unknowns in a pregnancy. You don't see what's going on inside so you may think you and the baby are fine, but there could be issues that only show up in an ultrasound."

Color leached out of Ryan's face. "What? Are you saying something's wrong? Are you having pain?"

Okay, so maybe expressing her concerns wasn't the right thing to do. "No, I don't think anything's wrong. I'm feeling great. But I'm a nurse, I know things."

Any more chance of conversation was halted when her doctor walked into the room.

"Good afternoon, how are you all today?" asked Dr. Jones her cheerfulness just what she needed.

"We're all good. How about you?" Suzie asked.

"Fine. Now are we looking forward to seeing your son or daughter again?"

"Yes." They both answered at the same time.

Dr. Jones smiled. "Excellent. Now have you decided if you'd like to find out the sex of the baby?"

Suzie started when the doctor smeared cool gel on her belly. Finding out the sex of the baby wasn't something they'd discussed. She looked at Ryan.

"Up to you," he murmured.

He continued to amaze her with how he let her make the important decisions. She knew it was must go against his nature as a person who has to make split second life and death situations in his job. He had to be in constant control and yet, he was handing it over to her.

Suzie turned back to Dr. Jones who was watching

them with an indulgent smile. "Yes. Yes, we'd like to find out."

"All right then. I'll take a few measurements and we'll listen to the heartbeat and then find out the sex of this baby. Sound good?"

"Sounds perfect." Ryan answered, his voice pitched low and the tone did crazy things to her heartbeat.

The next few minutes passed with the doctor moving the wand over her belly. Tears filled Suzie's eyes as the baby came into focus. A little hand waved in the air and both she and Ryan chuckled.

Ryan squeezed her hand so tight when the *whoosh whoosh whoosh* of their child's heartbeat filled the room.

"I don't think I'll ever get over how amazing that sound is," he said.

"It is a great sound and I have to say your baby looks strong and healthy. All the measurements are on spot for being twenty weeks pregnant. Okay, let's see if baby is going to cooperate and let us see the important part of this scan."

Suzie held her breath, unsure if she wanted a boy or a girl. Surely, a big tough Navy SEAL would want a son first. A boy to carry on his name.

"All right, baby is being cooperating and I can see what you're having."

Suzie squinted at the screen to see if she could work out between the black and grey lines what the sex of their baby was. Unfortunately, she couldn't tell. "What is it?" she asked tightening her already tight grip on Ryan's hand.

"Congratulations, you're having a daughter."

Her eyes flew to Ryan's hoping and praying she wouldn't see disappointment in them. What she saw had the tears filling her own eyes spilling over. He had the biggest smile she'd ever seen. "You're okay with having a girl?" she whispered.

Ryan leaned forward and kissed her quickly on the lips. "I couldn't be happier. Girls are precious. Thank you for gifting me with a daughter."

For the second time in a few hours, Suzie broke down crying in Ryan's arms, this time it was for joy and confirmed what she'd been trying to deny.

She would move in with Ryan. How could she not when she'd fallen head over heels in love with him?

Ryan would blast her if he was aware of where she was headed. It had been two weeks since her meltdown in her apartment. Between the two of them they'd managed to salvage one suitcase of clothes for her. Not that she could fit into them anymore. Her belly had well and truly popped and the news was out at work and within Ryan's team.

A little flutter of movement in her belly made her smile. She couldn't wait until she could dress her daughter in all the pretty girl's clothes she always admired when she walked past the baby section of department stores. So many dresses with ruffles and ribbons. Her smiled widened when she remembered how, after they'd left the doctor's surgery, Ryan stopped at a baby store and purchased a pink teddy bear. It took pride of place in the middle of their bed.

At first, she'd been angry with herself for craving his protection, but had slowly, with Ryan's help, come to the realization that moving in with him wasn't a show of weakness. He gave her all the space she needed, which wasn't much considering his place was a one-bedroom apartment. But he never forced her into anything and always asked her before he did anything.

With every passing second, she was falling more and more in love with him. The fear of him leaving again was forever imbedded in the back of her mind, but if he did, he'd already told her that Erin had offered her their spare room anytime she wanted it.

She pulled to a stop and looked up at the brown brick building. The day after her last visit to the apartment, Ryan had asked her if she was comfortable with him and a couple of the guys sorting out her apartment. At the time she never wanted to step foot into again, so she said yes. But over the last two days a restlessness she couldn't understand bit at her heels, encouraging her to see the place one last time before she handed the keys over to the buildings superintendent. The leasing company had been more than happy to let her out of her lease, without any penalty. For a second, she wondered if Ryan or even Tex had something to do with their acquiesce to her request to leave, but probably they were just happy she didn't sue.

"You can do this," she said out loud and the baby

kicked in agreement. "We're both strong independent women. We can face anything." She rubbed her belly once and then opened the door.

After a ride up the rickety elevator she, once again, stood outside her door. For the last time she inserted the key and opened it. Dust motes flew in the air, reminding her of the first time she'd opened the door after she'd signed her lease. Excitement had flowed through her then at her first step of independence. Now all she could think about was how it wasn't home. Home was with Ryan.

Before she could take a step, a hand clamped over her mouth and the chill of steel rested against her throat, stopping any thought of struggling out of the hold the person had on her. The blade was resting against her artery, one jolt and it would be sliced and she'd bleed out in a matter of minutes. Her hands instinctively went over her belly. She had a baby to protect and she would do whatever she needed to do to ensure nothing happened to her and Ryan's daughter.

"It's about time you came back here. I've been waiting. I knew you'd want to come back again." A low voice hissed in her ear. It sounded familiar, yet at the same time it didn't. "I'm just glad you didn't bring your boorish boyfriend. He's no good for you, my sweet Suzie. But I am. You belong to me. You always have."

By the time her assailant had finished speaking she worked out who it was. "Peter?" The word was muffled around the hand still covering her mouth.

"Got it in one, sweetheart. Now do you promise to be quiet?" To highlight his point, he pressed the knife harder against her neck.

Suzie nodded, there was more at stake here than her own safety. She had her daughter to think of and she would never put her at risk.

"Good girl." He removed his hand from her mouth waiting half a heartbeat before trailing it down her body. A shiver of revulsion filled her, and she struggled hard to stop the contents of her stomach landing at her feet. When Peter's hand connected with her baby bump she sucked in a deep breath. "Well. Well. Well. You have been busy haven't you. I was right, you are a slut."

"You broke into my apartment? Why? Why would you do that to me?"

"Oh no, you don't get to ask the questions. You've never had that right, don't you remember?" He didn't give her a chance to respond as the ding of the elevator arriving at her floor echoed down the hallway. The knife was removed from her throat and Peter's arm banded around her shoulder, pulling her tightly against him. The scent of his body odor assailed her nose and her stomach heaved again. How long had it been since he'd showered?

"Don't say a word," he muttered in her ear as he walked her down the hallway toward the stairwell.

"Suzie? Is that you?"

Oh no, Jeffrey. This was just getting worse. What if he and Peter were in cahoots together? Was this a plan conjured up between the two of them?

"Answer him, but if you give any indication of what is really going on here, I'm going to rip that kid out of your belly and watch the both of you die."

The venom in his voice indicated he meant every word he spoke. In all the time she'd been with Peter he'd never shown her this side. Apart from that one time when he'd struck her, he'd only verbally abused and controlled her. The man by her side was nothing like the man she'd known. He was truly insane.

Again she nodded, letting Peter know she understood his instructions. He turned them so she was facing her neighbor. "Hey Jeffrey, I was just paying the apartment one last visit before giving the super the key."

Her neighbor looked between her and Peter. She pasted a smile on her face, hoping it was convincing enough so he'd just continue on his way to his place and wouldn't get involved. "Where's your boyfriend?"

"We, uh, we broke up." Peter nudged in her ribs, a signal to finish the conversation. "Look, I've got to go. It's been great seeing you and thanks for being a good neighbor."

Peter didn't give Jeffrey a chance to respond as he turned her again and strode the short way to the stairwell. The slamming of the door filled the concrete space.

"You did well, sweetheart. Now let's go."

His fingers pinched into the soft flesh of her upper arm and he hurried her down the stairs. She gripped the railing to stop herself from tripping over her feet and slamming face first into the ground.

"Where are we going?" she asked when they pushed out into the bright sunshine.

"That's for me to know." They stopped beside a nondescript grey sedan. Peter opened the door and shoved her inside. "Don't try anything while I'm getting into the car."

As much as she'd like to make a run for it, the chances of her getting far away was slim. She pulled the seatbelt on and placed her hands on her belly. "It's okay, baby. Mommy's here and I'll not let anything happen to you."

"Aww isn't that sweet." He reached over and took her chin with his forefinger and thumb, pinching until her eyes watered at the pain. "You make me sick. Now it's time to sleep."

A sting pierced her upper arm, a pinprick of pain before lethargy spread through her, forcing her eyelids down.

I'm going to die. Her last thought before the blackness consumed her.

Quiet greeted him when Ryan opened the door to his apartment. Where was Suzie? She'd told him that morning before he'd left for PT that she had the day off and planned to do some window shopping, then come home and read her book.

He had no doubt, if she'd been called into work, she would've phoned or texted him to let him know.

His neck began to itch.

"Suzie?" He called out as he strode through the small place to their bedroom. Maybe she was sleeping. He looked through the doorway and saw the bed neatly made, her handbag missing from the small chair she rested it on when she got home from work.

"Fuck."

The itching increased.

It took him all of two minutes to check the apartment to find no trace of her. Her clothes were still in the closet, her toothbrush in the stand next to his, so she hadn't left him.

He dug into his pocket, pulled out his phone and dialed Suzie's number. It went straight to voicemail.

"Hey, Roses, it's me. Where are you? Are you all right? Call me when you get this?"

He fired off a text message as well. He paced around the room waiting for his phone to ring. After five minutes he dialed Italy's number. There was no way he was going to lose the woman he loved. And dammit, he *loved* Suzie and their daughter with all his heart. He couldn't imagine going the rest of his life without waking up beside her every morning. Seeing her beautiful face light up with a smile. Hearing her laugh while they watched a comedy together. No matter what, he was going to find Suzie and when he did he wasn't going to let her go. "Is Suzie with Erin?" Ryan asked the second the call was connected.

"No. Why?"

"She's not here."

Italy laughed. "Did she come to her senses and leave your sorry ass?" he joked.

"My neck is itching."

The laughter died immediately. "Fuck."

"Yeah."

Mentioning his sixth sense was all Italy needed to be told to know the situation was serious.

"Have you called, Tex?" he asked.

Ryan ran a face down his face, trying to control the panic welling inside of him. "No. Why would I call him?"

"Dude, you're not thinking straight. Calm down. I'll be there in ten minutes. In the meantime, call Tex."

Italy disconnected the call, not giving Ryan a chance to tell him not to bother coming over. Although that was a lie, he was grateful his friend and team mate was heading over.

Okay, what he needed to do was push his worry for Suzie to the back of his mind, not forgotten, but he needed to look at this situation logically, like he would when on a mission. Get the facts straight and then go from there. But first, he needed to do what Italy suggested and call Tex.

The former SEAL answered on the first ring. "Talk to me, Joker."

"I think Suzie's missing." Fuck, how lame did that sound.

"You think, or you know?"

"She's not home. She's not with Erin and my neck is itching."

"Right." In the background Ryan heard the distinctive sound of fingers flying over a keyboard. "When was the last time you saw her?"

"This morning at 0520 before I left for PT." More clicking.

"Was she working today?"

"No, she had the day off. Told me she was going to go window shopping and then come back home."

"Okay. Let's see if I can get some eyes on her trail," muttered Tex. Ryan began pacing as he let Tex do his stuff. The guy could find the proverbial needle in a field full of haystacks. "Bingo."

"What?" Ryan asked. "You've found her. Where is she?"

"Her car is parked outside her old apartment."

"What the hell?" A knock sounded on his door. He opened it and found all his teammates crowding the small hallway. He nodded, grateful for the show of support they were giving him. He waved them in. "What's she doing there? None of this makes sense. She told me she never wanted to go back to that place again."

"Well, that's where her car is. Looking through the footage from the cameras she got there around ten."

It was now after seven. She'd been there for almost ten hours. Like a bullet piercing a target a name burst into his head. "Jeffrey. I bet her disappearance has something to do with that fucker. No way is he going to hurt my girl. Thanks Tex." He disconnected the call, cutting off the other man.

"I know where she is," he said facing his teammates. "Let's go."

He was out the door and halfway to his car before Robot finally caught up with him. He went to grab his arm, but Ryan shook him off. His thoughts focused solely on getting to Jeffrey and wringing the fucker's neck until he got the information he needed.

"Joker! Stop now." Slowly through the red haze of anger enveloping him, Robot's command registered. Years of following orders from his superiors halted Ryan's mad progress to his car.

Robot and the rest of the team surrounded him. Each man looking serious but determined, letting him know he wasn't in this alone. They were with him every step of the way. It was exactly the same way they had approached the situation when Erin had been held captive. Only then they had Wolf's team with them. Plus, they knew where Erin was located. They only had speculation to go on as to Suzie's whereabouts.

Robot clapped his hand on his shoulder, applying enough pressure to let Ryan know he wouldn't be shaking off his team lead anytime soon. "I understand you want to get the fucker who's taken Suzie. I also understand that her being pregnant has you acting on emotion and not thinking this through. You can't go in all guns blazing. You *suspect* this Jeffrey is involved, you don't know it yet." Robot held up his hand when Ryan tried to interrupt him. "No, listen, we will do this the right way. This isn't a mission. Commander Black doesn't even know we're here. It's after seven in the evening. People will be home. Let's play this cool. We'll come up with a plan on the way to Suzie's last location. You understand?"

Ryan nodded. Everything Robot said was true. There was a reason he was the team lead. They split into two cars and made their way to Suzie's former apartment complex. Ryan's knee jerked up and down as Italy drove through the streets.

"It sucks doesn't it?" he said quietly.

"What?" asked Ryan.

"Knowing the woman you love is in trouble and you don't know where she is or what's she's going through."

"Yeah, I don't think the guy will hurt her. I think he's in love with her, too." He let out a harsh laugh. "Why wouldn't he be? Suzie is the best thing that ever happened to me. I need her, you know."

Italy's hands clenched the steering wheel and Ryan suspected he was reliving the moment when he heard the news that Erin and Antonia hadn't caught their flight. "Yeah, man, I get it."

"Did you say anything to Erin?" he asked, hoping inane conversation would keep his mind off finding Suzie hurt or worse. He squashed the thought before it could fully form in his mind.

"Yeah, I don't keep anything from her. She's worried but confident that we'll find her like we did her and Antonia."

Conversation drifted off and five minutes later they pulled to a stop a block away from the complex.

He exited the car and his adrenaline spiked at the impending confrontation.

"How are we going to do this," he asked when they met up with the rest of the team.

"Do you think you'll be able to knock on the guy's door and speak to him rationally about Suzie, or will one of us have to do it?" Robot asked.

"I can do it." He looked around at his team. "If you guys have my back."

"Always." They replied in unison.

"Okay," Robot continued. "We ask him if he's seen Suzie. The use of force will be kept to a minimum. Understand?"

The men all nodded, and Ryan pulled in on himself to get his mind in combat mode. It might not be combat like on a mission, but it was combat on getting his woman back. "Let's go," he said.

Together they walked toward the entrance of the building, all of them casing the surrounding area for anything out of the ordinary. He wondered if the rest of the guys were like him, wishing he had his weapon safely in his grip, ready to take action.

Once inside the building, Cowboy and Red took the stairs, while the rest of them took the elevator.

"This would have to be the slowest fucking elevator in history," T-Rex muttered.

"Tell me about it," responded Ryan, it was the exact same thought he'd had the first time he'd come and visited Suzie.

The cart ground to a halt and the doors slid open. "You take the lead, Joker. Italy will go with you,"

Robot said. "T-Rex and I will stay here to make sure nobody tries to take the elevator."

Ryan nodded. Their plan was solid they knew what they had to do and hopefully it would end peacefully and in a few minutes he'd have Suzie in his arms again. He planned on never letting her go.

The distance to Jeffrey's front door wasn't far but it may as well have been a ten mile trek through the jungles of the Congo with how long it seemed to take them to get to the eight foot high piece of wood.

Ryan's adrenaline amped up into overdrive the second they reached the door. He raised his fist to pound on it, but Italy's hand closed over his.

"I know you want pound the guy's face the second he opens the door, but what if he's not there. What if he's taken her someplace else? It wouldn't make sense to kidnap someone and then take them back to their own home. They'd take them to a place where no one would find them. It's what Bryan did with Erin and Antonia."

"I know. It doesn't make sense. But he's all I've got to go on. The way he's been acting around Suzie lately, he's bordering on being a stalker."

"Right, well let's do this calmly. Let me knock." Italy said and hit the wood. Ryan had to agree his knock was more *friendly* than Ryan's would've been.

He tapped his foot on the ground waiting for the door to open. A few seconds later it opened a crack. "What do you want?"

His whole demeanor was skittish, as though he was trying to hide something. Ryan clenched his fists at his side to prevent himself from pushing the door open and barging in. "I'm looking for Suzie? Her car's outside, is she here?"

"No." He went to shut the door, but Ryan palmed it preventing it from closing.

"Look, I know you like her, okay. But I love her and I'm worried. She's carrying my baby. I need to find her."

The last thing he planned to tell the guy was his feelings for Suzie, but he hoped, maybe, just maybe, it would be enough for Jeffrey to let him in. Or release Suzie to him.

"If you love her why did she break up with you?"

"What?"

"You heard me. She told me today she'd broken up with you."

This didn't make sense to Ryan. Why would Suzie tell Jeffrey that they'd broken up? When he'd left her this morning she was all warm and cozy in bed and he'd given her a hell of a goodbye kiss. It had taken the whole drive to PT for his erection to subside. What his words did do though, was confirm Jeffrey had seen her. At least they could be able to get a time-frame of when that happened, and her movements after her conversation with Jeffery. That is if Jeffrey wasn't her kidnapper. Ryan still wasn't sure the other man wasn't somehow involved in Suzie's disappearance.

"Please, Jeffrey, can we come in. I think she's in danger. I'm pretty sure you don't want anything to happen to her."

He contemplated Ryan's words for a few seconds before opening the door wider. A breath of relief whooshed out of him. Progress. That had to be a good thing.

He and Italy walked through the opening. The layout of Jeffrey's apartment was very similar to Suzie's. The area was as neat as a pin. The scent of lemon filled the air. A quick look around didn't unearth any hint that Suzie had been here. Not that a kidnapper would leave anything like that out in the open. If they did, they were pretty incompetent.

Once they sat down, Ryan leaned forward and clasped his hands together loosely between his legs. "When did you see Suzie?"

"Umm just after ten. I came home because I'd forgotten my lunch."

Studying the other man's body language for any hint he was lying wasn't difficult. It was something they'd been trained on. Everything indicated he was telling the truth. Ryan glanced at Italy who was leaning against the wall. He nodded at Ryan, confirming he believed Jeffrey wasn't lying either. To the untrained eye his stance looked relaxed, but Ryan knew his teammate was ready to spring into action at any time.

"Right. But you said Suzie told you we'd broken up?"

"Yes."

"You see I don't understand why she would do that. When I left her in bed this morning we were very much still together."

"Maybe you left the toilet seat up one time too many and so she decided enough was enough."

Ryan would've laughed but Jeffrey's stark one-eighty degree turn from affable to aggressive sent off warning bells.

"Do you know where she is? Is she here? Are you hiding her?"

The other man's shoulders slumped, as though the last smart-ass comment had taken all his bravado from him. "No. She isn't here. I…"

Out of the corner of his eye Ryan caught Italy standing up straighter. He'd heard the same waver in Jeffrey's voice that Ryan had too.

"You what?" Italy asked.

"I think you're right about her being in danger."

Ryan leaped up and in a flash Italy was by his side restraining him from grabbing the other man. "Joker, she's not here, okay. And I don't think he's involved," muttered Italy.

"Fine," he sat back down. Inwardly he agreed with his teammate. Jeffrey didn't display any signs of a man nervous about hiding something. Plus, apart from their arrival, he didn't seem eager to push them out the door.

"Jeffrey, as you can tell, Joker here is anxious to find his woman. If you've seen or heard anything that would be helpful, please share," asked Italy, his tone soothing and non-confrontational.

"I saw her leave with another man. He had his arm around her shoulder and when I asked why she wasn't with you…" He nodded his head toward Ryan. "She told me that you'd broken up."

The fact his prime suspect wasn't who he thought it was devastated Ryan. He had no idea now who had taken Suzie. He controlled the panic that was threatening to overwhelm him. He had to remember, if he let his emotions get the better of him, the chances of him finding Suzie was going to be slim. "Have you seen this person she was with before?"

"No. I haven't."

Fuck. He was hoping Jeffrey's need to know everything that happened in Suzie's life meant he'd seen every person that had knocked on Suzie's door. Which was ridiculous. Suzie worked all sorts of shifts. It was possible she had visitors when Jeffrey wasn't home.

"Can you describe him?" Italy asked.

"He was about your height," Jeffrey pointed at Italy. "He had dark hair and brown eyes."

"Did Suzie look like she wanted to be with him?" This time Ryan asked the question.

"No. She tried to look like she did, but she looked frightened and the guy had a tight grip around her shoulders."

Ryan almost wished it was Jeffrey that had taken Suzie. The guy sitting on the couch in front of him wouldn't hurt Suzie because he cared for her. But this person. The person he described as being with Suzie was someone who would like to hurt her.

"Fuck." He practically shouted the word as another suspect came to mind. "I can't believe I didn't think of this before."

"What?" Italy asked.

"Suzie's ex-husband. She told me about him just the other week."

"What about him?"

Ryan looked at his teammate. "She said he was verbally abusive to her. Controlling. I asked her if he could've been the one who trashed her apartment, but she said she didn't think so. She also mentioned that he'd hit her once, but she'd moved out after that."

"Bastard."

Ryan looked over at Jeffrey, surprised the word came out of his mouth.

"Any man who harms a woman is the scum of the earth. Women are meant to be treated like fine pieces of china. I would never hurt a woman." He looked up at Ryan, his eyes pleaded to for him to believe what he was about to say next. "I know you don't believe me, but I would never hurt Suzie. I will do anything to help you. Anything."

Ryan nodded. "I believe you and thank you. Do you think you'll be able to recognize the guy again if you saw a picture of him?"

"Without a doubt."

Ryan looked up at Italy who was already pulling his phone out of his pocket. "I'm texting the guys to come up here," he said. "You call Tex and see if he can find something out about Suzie's ex-husband."

Ryan reached into his own pocket and pulled out his cell. "On it." He punched in Tex's number.

"Whaddya need, Joker?"

He would've smiled at Tex's no-nonsense

approach if his heart wasn't beating out of his chest with worry. "I need you to look into Suzie's ex-husband. Her neighbor is clean, but he saw Suzie leave with a man. He says he could recognize him if he saw a picture."

"Right and you think this man Suzie left with was her ex?"

"Yeah, I do."

"On it. Give me five and I'll have a picture for you to show the other guy. Sit tight, Joker. We'll get your girl."

CHAPTER THIRTEEN

The binds around Suzie's wrists and ankles were chaffing and she badly needed to go to the bathroom. The last thing she wanted to do was ask Peter for anything, but she was desperate. "I need to use the bathroom. Can you please untie me?"

Peter, who was chewing on an apple while she sat with her stomach grumbling, looked up. "I don't know if you deserve to be released. What if you run away?"

Suzie bit down on the inside of her cheek to stop the smart retort she was bursting to release on him. The consequences of doing that could be catastrophic. Since their divorce he'd turned more violent, if what he did to her apartment was anything to go by. "Please, Peter, I promise not to run. Why would I? I've been miserable without you." The lie felt revolting on her tongue, but at this stage she would say and do anything to keep her and their baby safe.

"Doesn't look like it." He pointed his knife at her belly. "That says you've been having a good time."

"No, it was one night, and it was a mistake." Another lie, the night, and subsequent ones, were the best times she'd ever had. She wanted more of those best times with him. The only way that was going to happen was if she got out of there alive. Problem was she had no idea how she was going to do it. She only hoped that somehow Ryan knew she was missing and was working on a plan to release her.

She loved him, and she wanted to be able to tell him so. Wanted to squeeze his hand and yell at him as their daughter entered the world. Wanted to spend the rest of her life with him.

"Fine. I'll release you but don't try and do anything stupid while you're in the bathroom. Like squeezing through the window to try and escape."

Suzie snorted, she couldn't help it. The bathroom window was tiny and in her current pregnant state her ability to be able to fit through the small space was laughable. She couldn't believe that he'd brought her to their very first apartment they lived in. Had no idea he actually still had a lease for the place. "I told you. I'm not going anywhere." But she maybe she could find one of her old tube of lipsticks in the vanity. Maybe she could be able to write help on the window. It was a long shot, but she was desperate enough to try anything.

How she controlled a shudder of revulsion when he touched as he released the ropes around her wrists and ankles was beyond her. Pins and needles tingled through her extremities as the blood flowed back into them. She breathed through it and when she felt confident that she could make to the bathroom without collapsing she stood and walked slowly to the room.

The temptation to hide in the small room was huge, but the longer she lingered the more suspicious Peter would get. She completed her business and walked out, yelping when her wrist was grabbed.

"If you'd taken any longer I was going to come and get you."

"I'm sorry."

He harrumphed and marched her down the hallway. While they'd been married he'd never frightened her as much as he was doing right now. At present, Peter was so unstable she had no idea what he was capable of doing. Suzie prayed he wouldn't try and sleep with her. No way could she let that happen.

Peter paused and turned back to look at her. His eyes narrowing. She went to bite her lower lip but stopped herself. She'd always done that when she'd been hiding something from him. It was too late, he'd seen the movement.

"What did you do in the bathroom?" he demanded

"N-nothing."

He stalked toward her and she prayed with everything she had.

Please Ryan, work your magic and come save me. I need you... No, we *need you.*

At Robot's the group of men talked quietly waiting to hear back from Tex. Ryan paced around the space checking his phone every five seconds, which was completely stupid. The phone wasn't on silent. The second Tex called or texted he'd know it.

A hand clapped on his shoulder, he stopped and faced the owner. His jaw opened in surprise when he saw who was standing there. "Truck? What are you doing here? Shouldn't you be in Texas."

"Ghost and I were still in town and Tex called us. Where here to help anyway we can."

Ryan looked past the big Delta Force man and spied his team lead, Ghost talking to Robot. Having these two guys helping would be brilliant. While he and Truck had been traipsing through the jungle, Truck had filled him in on the history of the team and how most of them had all found love. Ghost's woman had been caught up in a hostage situation in Egypt. They'd saved her before she'd been raped.

"I'm grateful to the both of you for being here."

Truck nodded and when Ryan walked over to the window to gaze out into the darkness, the Delta Force man stood quietly beside him. He appreciated that Truck didn't try and make small talk.

A few minutes later Ryan's phone buzzed, he connected the call and hit speaker so everyone could hear. "What ya got for us, Tex?"

"Okay, I've done a little digging and I've found

where she is. You're right, Joker, she's with her ex, Peter Dulgrove."

Relief vied the with anger which swept through Ryan. Finally they had a solid lead. He hated to think of Suzie in the clutches of her ex again. "Do you know if she's safe?"

"Negative. There are no camera's in the building."

"How do you know she's there?"

"Because he's Tex," Truck said, as if those three words were all that he needed to understand.

"He found Erin. If he says he's located Suzie, then it's true."

Ryan let out a frustrated breath. "Sorry, brother, didn't mean to offend you.

"No offense taken. You're under stress. I get that."

The group listened as Tex went through the steps he'd taken to located Suzie. "You guys are going to have to do this by the book, I've notified the authorities, and pulled a few strings to ensure you guys get the job. They've given you an hour from when I contact them to tell them you're in position. If it's not done in that time, then they'll be sending in their own guys."

"We'll get it done," Ghost said, steel determination in his tone. "And we'll do it better than they ever can."

"I have no doubt. I'm sending you all the details I have on the building schematics. Let me know when you're in position."

"Will do," responded Ryan. He disconnected the

call and looked around at the assembled group. "Let's plan."

Thirty minutes later they were in position. Ryan was teamed up with Truck again. He'd been surprised when the other man had said he would have his back. If any of his teammates were upset with the idea, they didn't show it. And why would they, they weren't kids. At the end of the day they were working together as a team and that was all that mattered.

"Stairwell A, is secured." Robot's voice sounded in his ear.

"Eyes on the elevator," T-Rex confirmed.

"You ready?" asked Truck.

Ryan picked up the bag of food. "Yep."

It had appeared fate was looking down on them when Tex called back two minutes after they'd hung up saying Peter had called for Chinese takeout. They had their in. They were already in place when the delivery man arrived. Tex had worked his magic and the guy had handed over the bag—no questions asked.

"We're on the move," Truck said into the comms mic.

A chorus of affirmatives answered, and Ryan walked into the building, holding back the need to race up the stairs to the sixth floor and barge into apartment 615C.

The building was rundown. The foyer had peeling

wallpaper and faded carpet. The type of residents in this building wasn't the Martha Stewart type. They made their way over the elevator. Like the one in Suzie's building it was old and creaked the whole way up to the sixth floor.

Ryan was aware of Truck communicating with the rest of the team. His mind was focused only one thing—rescuing Suzie.

They reached the front door of the apartment where Suzie was being held. Truck took up his position out of view but able to strike if necessary. At his nod, Ryan rapped his knuckles on the door.

"Who is it?" A voice floated through the door.

"I've got your order from Golden Tiger Chinese."

"Leave it by the door. Here." The sound of something being pushed under the door had Ryan looking down—two one dollar bills were being shoved under the door. Wow, bigger tipper. But it presented a problem, they needed Peter to open the door.

"Sorry, Sir, but I can't do that. Golden Tiger's delivery policy states food cannot be left by the door. It must be handed over to the client."

"That's bullshit, just leave the fucking food and go away."

Okay, plan adjustment time. "Okay, Sir. Thank you for your business."

Ryan placed the food by the door and then started to walk down the hallway. Truck, understanding what he was doing, maintained his position. Peter would probably give it a few minutes before he opened the door and grabbed the food.

Crouching down low, he double backed and until he was standing behind Truck. Sure enough, the door opened cautiously and when a hand reached out to grab the food, Truck moved. Two seconds later Peter was on the ground, face smooshed into the dirty hallway carpet.

Ryan stepped over the man and rushed into the apartment. Over the comms he heard Truck alert the others he had Peter under control. He had no doubt the rest of his team would provide support if it was needed. All he wanted to do was find Suzie.

"Suzie!" The small, dirty living area was empty.

"Is she here?" Ryan turned to find Ghost and Robot standing a foot behind him.

"I don't know I only just walked in."

"If Tex said she's here. She'll be here," stated Ghost.

"Suzie?" he called again and held his breath, straining to hear anything to indicate his woman was in the apartment.

"There," said Ghost. "Do you hear it?"

A muffled thump sounded toward the back of the apartment. "Yes, let's go."

"Let me take the lead," Ghost said. "We don't know that he wasn't working with someone else. This is too easy."

Ryan couldn't deny the whole process had gone so easy. Truck and the rest of the team had subdued Peter. Just because it had gone off without a hitch didn't mean it was a bad thing. Sometime missions worked out that way. "I've got your back, Ghost."

Together they made their way down the hallway, waiting for another thump to sound. They paused outside a door. A second later they heard a faint whimper.

His heart skipped a beat at the sound.

"Control yourself man," Ghost whispered as he pulled out a glock he had in the back of his trousers, turning the safety off. "On the count of three." He held up three fingers, lowering them one at a time.

When the final digit dropped, Ryan readied himself for whatever was lurking behind the door. Ghost went in gun aimed straightforward, no sooner had he crossed over the threshold he called to Ryan. "Joker, in here now."

Trusting that Ghost would cover him if the need arose, Ryan marched through the opening, his heart dropping to his feet at what he saw. In the middle of the bed lay Suzie, eyes swollen shut, blood trickling from cuts above her eye and the corner of her mouth. "Fuck, Suzie." He rushed over to her side, controlling his instinct to haul into his arms.

"I'm gonna get Truck, don't move her," Ghost ordered.

"Get Cowboy too, he's the medic on our team," Ryan countered as he carefully climbed on to the bed next to her. His fingers trembled as he brushed some hair away from her face. He leaned close to murmur in her ear. "I'm here, Roses. I'm never going to let you go, do you understand me. I'm so sorry I didn't keep you safe, again. Please don't leave me. I need you." His voice broke on the final words.

"Ryan." His name a mere whisper on a breath.

"Yeah, baby, it's me."

"Baby."

Terror paralyzed him, Suzie had suffered a beating, her face all the evidence he needed. If the fucker of her ex-husband had harmed their unborn child, Ryan was going to make him pay.

He ran his hands down her body, feeling the hard swell of their child. Ryan lightly pressed his hand on her belly, willing their child to answer the nudge he gave her with an answering kick. Only there wasn't one. He wanted to try again but was too scared in case he hurt their daughter. He kept his hands on Suzie's belly, waiting and willing for any sign their child was going to be all right.

"Joker, let me check her out," Truck's quiet voice reached him.

He looked up at Truck, tears blurring his scarred face. "She's not kicking back."

CHAPTER FOURTEEN

The edge of the plastic chair dug into the back of Ryan's legs. He'd been sitting in it for five minutes after Robot told him to sit the fuck down. He'd been pacing around the waiting room of the hospital like a caged tiger ever since the doctor kicked him out of the emergency cubicle Suzie had been put in.

"It's going to be all right, Ryan. Suzie's one tough lady and so is your baby. How could it be anything else? It's part Navy SEAL."

Erin's voice broke through his thoughts. He looked up and smiled, glad she was here. In fact, the whole team, including Ghost, Truck and Antonia, were all in the waiting room with him. A sense of *deja vu* had rippled through him. It wasn't too long ago they were all here for Erin and Antonia, waiting on news. The day he met Suzie. The day his life changed. "I don't think I ever thanked you for being there for Suzie when her place was broken into and for letting her stay with you while I was away."

Erin waved his words off. "It was nothing. She's family and, after talking to Caroline, Wolf's wife, we girls need to stick together when you boys are away."

He swallowed against the lump in his throat. Erin was right, they were family and proof of that was how, in times of trouble, they were all there for each other.

"You are insufferable." Antonia's voice echoed around the room and Ryan looked up to see her glaring at Robot before walking out. After glaring at her departing back, few seconds later Robot followed.

"What is going on with those two?" he asked Erin.

"No idea, Antonia is still refusing to answer my questions."

Before he could comment a doctor walked through the door. He scanned the room, clearly used to the sight of muscled military men. "I'm looking for a Ryan Smith."

Ryan shot to his feet. "That's me. How's Suzie… and the baby? Are they okay?"

"Ms. Waterson has suffered cuts and bruises on her face, fortunately she didn't suffer any fractures to her face. However, she has two cracked ribs, so she will be in pain for a while. With regards to her pregnancy," he paused, and Ryan's heart stopped beating. He didn't want to hear what the doctor had to say next. He felt, more than saw, his teammates congregate behind him, giving him their support. "All tests show that there are no visible tears in the amniotic sac and the baby's heartbeat is still strong. We will need to monitor her closely as there was a small amount of bleeding, but we don't believe there will be any lasting effects. From the bruising on her arms and back it appears she did everything she could to protect her child."

Ryan had no doubt Suzie's only thought was protecting their daughter. His woman would do everything to ensure the safety of their child, just like he would do for them. The urgency he'd been keeping at bay flooded him. He had to see for himself that Suzie was okay. Had to hold her. Lay his hand over their daughter to reassure himself that all was right in his world. "Can I see her?"

"We're getting her transferred to a room. Once she's settled I'll get a nurse come to see you. Rest assured, Mr. Smith, Suzie is one of ours, she'll get the best care possible."

The doctor acknowledged the group and strode out of the room. Ryan's breath whooshed out of him and a million emotions swamped him. He registered the sound of someone crying. Only when a pair of arms slid around him, did it hit him—he was the one crying.

"It's okay, Joker, they're both okay," Erin murmured into his shoulder. He allowed himself a few moments to seek comfort from Erin, before pulling himself together and clearing his throat.

"Thanks."

Robot came up. "I thought you should know that Peter has been charged with assault and kidnapping.

The police will want to talk to Suzie about what she went through."

"They'll just have to wait. She's not going to be talking to anyone about this until the doctor clears her and there's no risk the stress of remembering her ordeal will hurt her and our daughter."

"Understood. I'll let them know." He then canted his head toward the door. "Looks like your escort is here. Go see your girl."

Five minutes later Ryan was seated beside Suzie's bed, her baby bump a welcome sight. He placed one of his hands over his daughter and held Suzie's hand with his other. A little jolted lifted his hand resting on her belly.

Then another.

For the first time in hours his lips widened into a genuine smile. "Hey sweetheart, this is your daddy. I'm going to keep you and your mommy safe. Do you hear me. I love you and I love your mom. Now I want you to stay there, all nice and warm, until it's time for you to meet us." He leaned forward and kissed her belly through the blankets.

"You're going to make a great dad."

Ryan closed his eyes for a few seconds savoring the sound of Suzie's husky, sleep laden voice. The best sound he'd ever heard. He swallowed pushing down the lump of emotion, before sitting up and looking at Suzie. "Hey, Roses." Needing to reassure himself that she definitely was fine he pushed back the chair, giving him more room to touch his lips to hers, careful not to hurt her battered skin. "Can I get you anything?" he asked as he sat down again, clasping her hand in both of his.

Her own hand drifted down to her stomach. "She really is okay?"

"Yep, the doctor said there doesn't appear to be any damage to her but they're going to keep you on bedrest for a few days to be sure. You're a fierce Mama, you protected her and kept her safe. You're going to be an amazing Mom."

She smiled at how he changed the words she'd spoken to him about being a good dad. She went to move but winced. "Ouch."

Having suffered from fractured ribs himself he was well aware of how the slightest movement could cause shooting pain. "It's going to take a little while to heal but I promise not to tell silly jokes."

"Apart from the first night we met I don't think you've told me one joke."

Ryan thought back over their relationship since she walked back into his life, in a room very similar to the one she was in. Suzie was right. He hadn't told her any lame jokes, as was the norm with him. He should've worked out that Suzie was his soulmate. He didn't have to prove who he was or try to be someone else. He could be himself and not worry about being judged. "Yeah, I haven't."

Silence settled around them. Ryan was waiting for the questions he could tell Suzie wanted to ask. He would wait until she was ready. He wouldn't force her to relive her ordeal.

Her fingers squeezed his. "Is Peter still alive?"

So not the question he thought she'd ask, but then again, perhaps it was. "Yeah, he's in police custody charged with assault and kidnapping. The police want to question you, but I told Robot to tell the cops they're not to speak to you until the doctor clears you."

She nodded and processed what he told her. "How did you find me?"

"Tex."

"I should've known," she said, a small smile playing across her lips. "If the guy could call me five minutes after I called the cops about my break-in, make sense he'd be able to find me."

"The guy is a whizz and I'm really glad he's on our team. He found your car at your old apartment complex. I thought Jeffrey had finally cracked and had taken you."

Suzie licked her lips, and he released his hold on her and grabbed the cup of water resting on the table by the bed. He held the straw to her lips and she took some swallows. "It wasn't Jeffrey."

"I know, but he helped us. He told us that he'd seen you and once I worked out that it could've been your ex, I called Tex and he was able to pull a picture up. We showed Jeffrey and he confirmed he was the man he saw you with." Ryan breathed out, releasing the tension remembering the anxiety filling him while they waited for Tex to get a picture of Peter. But it was all over, and his family was safe. "After that, Tex did what Tex does best and we found you."

"Since I left Peter," she paused. Her mouthing

opening and closing a couple of times as if trying to gather her thoughts. "I've needed to be independent and in control of my life. When he stuck the knife against my neck all I wanted to do was relinquish control and have you come rescue me. Does that make me weak?" Tears pooled in her eyes. It crushed him to see them.

"Oh Roses, no it doesn't make you weak at all. And, even though you may not think it you were in control. You kept yourself safe until we could get to you."

"I suppose." Her eyelids drifted down.

"Sleep now. I'll be here when you wake up."

"Promise?" she murmured.

Ryan raised her hand to his lips and brush a soft kiss across her knuckles. "I promise. I love you, Roses."

Her lips curved into a smile, the only indication she'd heard what he said to her.

Suzie woke and winced as she attempted to stretch. The room was darker than it had been the first time she'd woken up.

"Hey, how are you feeling? Do you need anything?" Ryan's soft voice filled her with warmth, and the words he'd spoken before she fell asleep floated across her brain.

Did he really say he loved her?

With all her heart, she hoped she'd heard him

correctly. Her love for him had been what kept her strong while Peter had her. She'd believed that he would find her, and he had.

"Do you really love me?" she asked, surprising herself with the question.

With careful movements he climbed on the narrow hospital bed beside her. He cupped her face and looked deeply into her eyes. Her breath caught at the light shining in them. "Aww Suzie, yes I do. I love you with me whole heart. You are my world. If anything had happened to you, I don't know what I would've done." His voice broke and a single tear trickled out of the side of his eye.

The sight had her own eyes filling up. Her big, tough Navy SEAL was showing her a side of him she was sure he kept hidden. She wiped away the tear. "I love you too, Ryan."

Her heart stuttered as his lips stretched into a wide smile. "Thank God," he muttered and lowered his lips to caress hers in a soft kiss.

The lack of room and her sore ribs made it impossible for her to twist fully in his embrace. An embrace she never wanted to ever leave.

Ryan broke the kiss and smiled at her. "Do you love me enough to marry me?"

When she'd walked out on Peter, Suzie imagined she'd walk through life alone. But then a group of Navy SEALs marched into her hospital and one captured her heart, with his lame jokes and cheeky smile. She should've known she her heart was about to be captured the moment she said yes to his dinner date. "Yes. Yes, Ryan *Joker* Smith I will marry you. But I'm not going to look like a whale. Our marriage will have to wait until after our daughter enters the world."

"Whatever you want." He rested his forehead against hers. "You're in total control."

EPILOGUE

Suzie rubbed her belly wishing baby Smith would hurry up and make her entrance into the world.

"How many more days?" asked Erin, rubbing her own belly.

What was it about pregnant women that it was natural to rub circles over their belly? Suzie found herself doing so every chance she got. What she loved more was when Ryan rubbed cocoa butter over her belly at the end of the day.

"Ten but who's counting," Suzie joked.

"I like your place? But I think you're insane having a house warming party so close to the baby being born."

"Ryan wanted to share it with all the guys and," she blushed as she remembered exactly how her man convinced her to have the party. "I couldn't say no."

Erin laughed out loud. "I know that look. I'm pretty sure I've had that cross my face a few times."

"You have," muttered Antonia as she walked into the kitchen. "The hormones flying around this room is disgusting. I have no idea why I moved here. Being surrounded by you lovesick fools is annoying."

Erin tapped her friend on the arm. "Who are you trying to fool? You love living here. You just need to find yourself a man. There's plenty out there?" Erin waved her arm to the display of hunky Navy SEALs all standing around the grill.

Suzie observed the way Antonia's eyes arrowed in on Robot who was teaching Ryan the finer points of flipping a steak.

"I don't think so," Antonia said as she turned on her heel and walked out the room.

Suzie raised her eyebrows at Erin. "Those two just need to go find a room and work things out."

"I think they've done that on more than one occasion." Erin mused. Then her face lit up as Carlos waved at her. "I've given up trying to work out what's going on with Robot and Antonia. But they need to figure things out. The tension between the two of them is crazy and makes gatherings like this a little uncomfortable."

"Yep," Suzie looked out the kitchen window just as Ryan was looking at her. She blew him a kiss. God, she loved that man.

"It's good to see you both so happy," Erin commented.

"Ryan was telling me the guys are giving him a hard time cause he's always smiling."

Erin laughed. "Yeah, Carlos said the same after we got together. Have you met the girl who came with T-Rex?"

"Briefly when they arrived but then I came in here to sort out the food. Have you talked to her?"

"Not really, he seems rather protective of her. Carlos met her once before. There's a story there, but it's not mine to tell."

Suzie nodded. "I'll make sure I go see her once things settle down."

"Sounds good. Carlos is waving to me like a madman, will you be okay if I go see him?"

Suzie laughed. "Sure, I'll be fine."

After Erin left, she went to the refrigerator and pulled out the salad she'd prepared, almost dropping it when warm arms slid around her waist and a pair of decadent lips nipped at her neck.

"Hey there, Roscs."

She replaced the bowl and turned in Ryan's embrace, looping her arms around his neck. "Hey there, Joker."

He smiled as she teased him by calling him by his nickname. She didn't do it often, but today, with all his teammates around him it seemed the thing to do. His lips descended on hers in a wild and wicked kiss. Even though she was about to pop, one kiss from her man, had desire leaping through her veins. "How soon can we get them to leave?" she asked when Ryan broke the kiss.

He laughed, a sound she never tired of hearing. "We have to feed them, but after that, I'm all for kicking them out."

"Have I told you how much I love you?"

"Yes, and I love you, too. So much." At that second their daughter made her presence known by kicking them both. "Yes, sweetheart, I love you, as well."

When his lips closed over hers again, Suzie melted in his arms, feeling safe and loved like she never had before. Life didn't get much better than this.

If you enjoyed this book please consider leaving a review. All reviews are greatly appreciated.

JOIN my Newsletter and find out about sales, free books, contests and new releases before anyone else!! Click HERE

You can read the first book in the series Guarding Erin. Click HERE

Don't miss Protecting Maria. Grab your copy today. Click NOW

To find out about new releases and sales follow me on Bookbub. Follow me

ABOUT THE AUTHOR

On her very first school report her teacher said 'Nicole likes to tell her own stories'. Many years later she eventually sat down and wrote her first book.

Nicole writes sexy contemporary romances, seducing you one kiss at a time as you turn the pages. She enjoys taking two characters and creating unique situations for them.

Learn more about Nicole Flockton at http://www.nicoleflockton.com.

authornicole@nicoleflockton.com

ACKNOWLEDGMENTS

As always thank you to Susan Stoker and her readers for making me feel so welcome in this world. I love revisiting Susan's characters and weaving them into my stories. It's so much fun playing in this world

As special thank you to Kathy Espitia and Rebecca Arnett-Velez for helping me come up with Suzie ex-husband's name. And thank you to everyone who answered my call for help with some great suggestions.

Thank you to Abigail Owen, my cheerleader, my beta reader and my friend. Doing writing sprints with you is such and fun, and are a main reason my word count has increased.

To Wren Michaels, I love our coffee mornings – well you drink the coffee! You've been with me on this journey since I signed my very first contract and I can't thank you enough for your friendship and love.

To Jennifer from More than Words Promotions, your skill with bringing my covers to life is amazing. You took this picture and made him Joker! Having you on my team is a blessing.

Speaking of teams, I couldn't do this without the unfailing support of my family. Jason, Skylar and Zane I can't express how much I love you guys. You're my world. Thank you all for supporting me as I pursue my dreams.

ALSO BY NICOLE FLOCKTON

Guardian Seals Series

Protecting Lily

Protecting Maria

Guarding Erin

Guarding Suzie

Guarding Brielle

The Elite

Fighting to Win

Fighting to Dream

Fighting for Love

Fighting for Redemption

The Freemasons

The Victor

The Hunter

Sweet Texas Secrets

Sweet Texas Fire

Sweet Texas Series Boxed Set

Bound Series

Bound by Her Ring

Bound by His Desire

Bound by Their Love

Bound by The Billionaire's Desire - Boxed Set

Lovers Unmasked Series

Lovers Unmasked: The Complete Series

Masquerade

Rescuing Dawn

Seducing Phoebe

Emerald Springs Legacy Series

Daniel's Decision

Emerald Springs Legacy Collection

Standalone Titles

White Knight (Co-Written with Abigail Owen)

Novellas

Tangled Vines

Melt My Heart Anthology

Tango Love

A Vacation Affair

Medal Up: A Winter Games Duology

Swipe for Mr. Right

Wrong Time for Mr. Right

As you know, this book included at least one character from Susan Stoker's books. To check out more, see below.

Delta Force Heroes Series

Rescuing Rayne (FREE!)
Rescuing Aimee (novella)
Rescuing Emily
Rescuing Harley
Marrying Emily
Rescuing Kassie
Rescuing Bryn
Rescuing Casey
Rescuing Sadie
Rescuing Wendy
Rescuing Mary (Oct 2018)
Rescuing Macie (April 2019)

Badge of Honor: Texas Heroes Series

Justice for Mackenzie (FREE!)
Justice for Mickie
Justice for Corrie
Justice for Laine (novella)
Shelter for Elizabeth
Justice for Boone
Shelter for Adeline
Shelter for Sophie
Justice for Erin
Justice for Milena
Shelter for Blythe

Justice for Hope (Sept 2018)
Shelter for Quinn (Feb 2019)
Shelter for Koren (June 2019)
Shelter for Penelope (Oct 2019)

SEAL of Protection Series

Protecting Caroline (FREE!)
Protecting Alabama
Protecting Fiona
Marrying Caroline (novella)
Protecting Summer
Protecting Cheyenne
Protecting Jessyka
Protecting Julie (novella)
Protecting Melody
Protecting the Future
Protecting Kiera (novella)
Protecting Dakota

SEAL of Protection: Legacy Series

Securing Caite (Jan 2019)
Securing Sidney (May 2019)
Securing Piper (Sept 2019)
Securing Zoey (TBA)
Securing Avery (TBA)
Securing Kalee (TBA)

New York Times, *USA Today* and *Wall Street Journal* Bestselling Author Susan Stoker has a heart as big as the state of Texas where she lives, but this all American girl has also spent the last fourteen years living in Missouri, California, Colorado, and Indiana. She's married to a retired Army man who now gets to follow *her* around the country.

She debuted her first series in 2014 and quickly followed that up with the SEAL of Protection Series, which solidified her love of writing and creating stories readers can get lost in.

If you enjoyed this book, or any book, please consider leaving a review. It's appreciated by authors more than you'll know.

www.stokeraces.com
www.AcesPress.com
susan@stokeraces.com

More Books in the Special Forces: Operation Alpha World!

Brynne Asher: Blackburn
Denise Agnew: Dangerous to Hold
Shauna Allen: Awakening Aubrey
Shauna Allen: Defending Danielle
Shauna Allen: Rescuing Rebekah
Shauna Allen: Saving Scarlett
Shauna Allen: Saving Grace
Jennifer Becker: Hiding Catherine
Julia Bright: Saving Lorelei
Victoria Bright: Surviving Savage
Victoria Bright: Going Ghost
Victoria Bright: Jostling Joker
Kendra Mei Chailyn: Beast
Kendra Mei Chailyn: Barbie
Kendra Mei Chailyn : Pitbull
Melissa Kay Clarke: Rescuing Annabeth
Melissa Kay Clarke: Safeguarding Miley
Samantha A. Cole: Handling Haven
Samantha A. Cole: Cheating the Devil
Sue Coletta: Hacked
KaLyn Cooper: Rescuing Melina
Liz Crowe: Marking Mariah
Jordan Dane: Redemption for Avery
Jordan Dane: Fiona's Salvation
Riley Edwards: Protecting Olivia
Riley Edwards: Redeeming Violet
Nicole Flockton: Protecting Maria

Nicole Flockton: Guarding Erin
Nicole Flockton: Guarding Suzie
Nicole Flockton: Guarding Brielle
Casey Hagen: Shielding Nebraska
Casey Hagen: Shielding Harlow
Casey Hagen: Shielding Josie
Desiree Holt: Protecting Maddie
Kathy Ivan: Saving Sarah
Kathy Ivan: Saving Savannah
Kathy Ivan: Saving Stephanie
Jesse Jacobson: Protecting Honor
Jesse Jacobson: Fighting for Honor
Jesse Jacobson: Defending Honor
Jesse Jacobson: Summer Breeze
Silver James: Rescue Moon
Silver James: SEAL Moon
Silver James: Assassin's Moon
Becca Jameson: Saving Sofia
Kate Kinsley: Protecting Ava
Heather Long: Securing Arizona
Heather Long: Guarding Gertrude
Heather Long: Protecting Pilar
Heather Long: Covering Coco
Kirsten Lynn: Joining Forces for Jesse
Margaret Madigan: Bang for the Buck
Margaret Madigan: Buck the System
Margaret Madigan: Jungle Buck
Margaret Madigan: December Chill
Rachel McNeely: The SEAL's Surprise Baby
Rachel McNeely: The SEAL's Surprise Bride
KD Michaels: Saving Laura

KD Michaels: Protecting Shane
Wren Michaels: The Fox & The Hound
Wren Michaels: The Fox & The Hound 2
Wren Michaels: Shadow of Doubt
Wren Michaels: Shift of Fate
Wren Michaels: Steeling His Heart
Kat Mizera: Protecting Bobbi
Mary B Moore: Force Protection
LeTeisha Newton: Protecting Butterfly
LeTeisha Newton: Protecting Goddess
LeTeisha Newton: Protecting Vixen
LeTeisha Newton: Protecting Heartbeat
MJ Nightingale: Protecting Beauty
MJ Nightingale: Betting on Benny
MJ Nightingale: Protecting Secrets
Sarah O'Rourke: Saving Liberty
Debra Parmley: Protecting Pippa
Lainey Reese: Protecting New York
Jenika Snow: Protecting Lily
Jen Talty: Burning Desire
Jen Talty: Burning Kiss
Jen Talty: Burning Skies
Jen Talty: Burning Lies
Megan Vernon: Protecting Us
Megan Vernon: Protecting Earth

Made in the USA
Lexington, KY
23 August 2018